A Long Journey:
Steam to Cyber

Gracie Stathers

© Gracie Stathers 2017
Edited by Jenny Argante
Proofread by Shona Barnett
Cover design by Sufi of Delphi Designz

ISBN   978-0-473-38302-2   (p/b)

Wallace Publishing NZ
Villa 2
30 Carmichael Road
Bethlehem
Tauranga 3110
New Zealand-Aotearoa

Author's Note

I am proud to disclose I am a sixth-generation New Zealander descended from ancestors who travelled from Europe for various reasons and settled in the French town of Akaroa.

I believe this is what gave me the desire to tell some of the stories that make up the history of our beautiful country, and to share some of the anecdotes I've heard within my own family.

Over the years I have observed that these family storytellers were firmly of the belief that you should never let the truth stand in the way of a good story.

I have followed their excellent example.

For a more truthful account, contact me at
graciestathers@gmail.com

To Families

Part 1:
Transportation

'What is the fire in our belly but the eternal flame of a thousand ancestors?'

Robert Brault

Chapter 1

Datchworth village in England, 1845

Edward Cole was in the habit of attending All Saints Church every Sunday.

He admired the old fourteenth-century building with its combination of local stone and flint; parts had been added over the years as finances or necessity dictated. This morning Edward walked through the new porch, which led him to a fine entrance arch, then down the aisle to take his seat. His eyes settled on the fifteenth-century font with its elaborate workmanship.

The font was a recent addition that Edward had helped to purchase. The panelled stem, intricately carved, flowed towards the octagonal bowl it supported. The ornate lid of brass, with contrasting black spirals scrolling upwards, took the eye towards the stained glass windows that featured Moses and Elijah in the wilderness.

He understood that the windows brought peace to

the parishioners who knew the Bible stories of temptation, betrayal and triumph through faith, but for Edward the church was a place to rest rather than worship. He was not a devout man, though he tried to live by the biblical principle of 'doing unto others as you would have them do unto you.'

He seated himself next to his elderly parents at the front of the church; his was a family of some importance in the village. The poorest parishioners sat at the back, in attendance because of social pressure rather than by choice. In sufferance, they listened to the sermons that delivered a message that would do nothing to fill their empty bellies.

Sunday dinner at Edward's house was a grand affair. His housekeeper insisted on keeping up appearances at least on this one day of the week. Mrs Ellis was a short, fleshy woman, always cheerful and content to follow Edward's instructions on week days.

"Plain meals with no fuss," he would tell her. But on Sundays when Edward's parents came to dine, she set out fine cutlery and crystal glasses on the long dining table with its crisp white tablecloth, and served pigeon pie, venison or salmon with vegetables, and cake and tarts to follow.

The dining room was small and intimate, made to look larger by a gilded mirror hanging on the wall opposite Edward's chair. A beautifully decorated timber sideboard showed off fine pieces of china which reflected light from candles in the chandelier hanging low over the table. The crystal glasses sparkled as though to emphasise the contrasting dark red wine and the white-painted room.

Edward was an only child; tall and a little too slim, yet handsome. He took care of his appearance, and today his jacket was a fashionable black velvet with gold buttons. His waistcoat of white brocade had a high collar that swept up over a white silk cravat, showing to advantage the slender neck rising to a strong, well-angled jaw.

The talk around the table on Sundays always centred on the local gossip, a habit that did not sit well with Edward; conversation full of prejudice and misunderstandings brought about by his parent's determination to cling to old beliefs which held them captive. They had little understanding of the issues that their son was dealing with in his position at the Assizes.

Edward had made the choice to work for his living instead of relying on family money. He found it rewarding to have a reason to get out of bed in the morning. His employment kept him in touch with what was going on in the village and the plight many of the villagers were facing; he had been involved with the justice system long enough to know there was trouble ahead.

This year more convicts than ever before were being sent to Norfolk Island. Edward believed this increase was a drive towards colonisation rather than retribution for crimes. The country was caught up in a flourish of industrialisation at home and colonisation abroad, a policy that cared little for its effects on the population.

Norfolk Island had come in for special attention recently - and not for the first time - with rumours spreading about the harsh conditions. Edward tried to speak with his parents about his concerns and the need for something to be done in a situation, he predicted, would end in tragedy.

He explained to them how, five years previously, Captain Alexander Maconochie had brought some good changes to the island

"Maconochie was a compassionate man, who believed the convicts deserved a chance to rehabilitate. He set up a points system that gave the prisoners an opportunity to better themselves."

But his parents down-played this good work in favour of the more sordid news that had been circulating of sodomy among the prisoners, and riots. This confirmed their belief that the prisoners were deserving of the lash and other deterrents. Edward knew this was what most people preferred to believe;

much would need to be done to change such views.

Captain Maconochie had made a difference with his new system, even though he got little support from his supervisors nor from the constables, many of whom were ex-convicts. Fourteen hundred men earned their freedom during the experimental system.

Unfortunately, there was a darker side to Maconochie. The strong Presbyterian influence in his upbringing would not allow him to disregard what he considered the unnatural act of sodomy. For this crime, he turned to the lash with more fervour than anyone before him. The average number of lashes rose to ninety-three. These were the rumours that festered in the dining rooms of England.

Edward had followed with interest the man who had taken the place of Maconochie, Major Joseph Childs, who was, like his predecessor, a Navy man - but without the constraints of the church. Childs, used to dealing with highly disciplined men, did not cope well with the undisciplined and desperate men of Norfolk Island. Maconochie had encouraged the convicts to set up trading among themselves but under Childs' leadership the scheme led to the formation of gangs of bullies.

By the time Childs had reached the end of his two-year reign he had left most of the day to day running of the colony to subordinate officers and supervisors who did nothing to discourage the actions of these bullies.

A decision was made to recall Childs and replace him with someone with 'better judgement and firmness'.

Edward was fully aware of the story behind the chosen replacement, a man who seemed far too familiar with the working of the criminal mind to be put in charge of convicts; John Giles Price was different from the other commanders because he was a civilian, the fourth son of Sir Rose Price. He had studied at Oxford and was able to obtain letters of introduction from influential relatives. He used these to advantage when he moved to Van Diemen's Land, where he met and married Mary, the daughter of James Franklin and ward of Sir John Franklin, the Lieutenant-Governor.

When Price was appointed Muster-Master of the convicts, a shameful period was soon to begin.

After the meal was over Edward's mother, a graceful woman who kept herself fit and healthy, rose from the table and peeked out the window to check on the weather.

"Why don't we take a walk to while away the

afternoon?" she suggested.

The December day was cold but pleasant and Edward decided the fresh air might blow away the melancholy that had overcome him of late. Edward's father preferred to read his book beside the fire, so mother and son donned hats and wrapped themselves in scarves to walk out together.

They passed the old whipping post, disused now for nearly two hundred years, and then the stocks that Edward believed were a more appropriate punishment for petty crime than the recent system of transportation. They passed the church and burial grounds and spoke of the morning's sermon, centred on Ephesians 5:31: "A man leaves his father and mother and is joined to his wife and the two are united as one."

"It is time you found a new wife, Edward. Is there no one who takes your fancy?"

Edward did not answer straight away, silenced by the deep sadness that swept over him like a tidal wave. How could he tell his mother there was someone; in fact, always had been, even before he had married his betrothed.

Edward's wife Annette was fair of face and proved to be a 'suitable and dutiful' partner who had tried to bring him happiness. But it wasn't possible for any wife to quell the flame that burned within him for the woman of his desire. Annette had conceived early in their marriage. The pregnancy went well, but neither she nor the infant survived the birth.

Even though it was more than a year since he had been widowed, Edward still felt somehow responsible for the two deaths. The mysteries of childbirth were beyond his understanding, something he could not control. Those who comforted him gave assurance that even a young and healthy woman could be taken in childbirth.

Edward could not understand how a baby as perfect as the child he had held in his arms did not even take her first breath. He would never know whether the child could have healed the sadness in his heart or curbed the constant yearning for a love he could never have.

Now he answered his mother simply, "perhaps, in time."

The pair walked on in silence and soon Edward's thoughts turned to the one hundred and ninety-nine prisoners he had prepared for boarding the ship named *Mayda*, which had sailed for Norfolk Island four months earlier.

What must it be like to put to sea for the first time and sail away from family and friends, never to return?

Edward had known four of the men who had been

sentenced, all of them from one family in this village. Hard-working men with wives and children to provide for, and yet he had helped to prepare them to be bundled onto a ship sailing for five months to the other side of the world.

Four women were left behind to fend for themselves and raise their babies at a time when society was changing rapidly. If it was hard for any family to put food on the table, it was almost impossible for a woman on her own.

One hundred and ninety-nine men lined up waiting to board the convict ship *Mayda*. Only five of them were married, and four of those were of the Shadbolt family from the village of Datchworth.

There were others boarding with well-known names such as Smith and Jones, but none of them were related; it was unusual, indeed, for so many men from one family to be sent from their homes.

The four named Shadbolt had said goodbye to the ones they would leave behind, through cold narrow bars in prison doors. Each vowed to be strong, but now as they stood for their final minutes on home soil, they felt the numbness of separation, and the chilling fear of the unknown gnawing through them like mice chewing through cork.

They had all heard stories about Norfolk Island; a place chosen to deport the worst criminals from the British Isles; a place where men were subjected to the harshest of punishments; not a place for married men with families. Each of the Datchworth men was sentenced to fifteen years, almost time for their children to grow up and have families of their own, before they were released.

The Shadbolts had made a pact with their wives, agreeing the women must be free to find another husband to bring food to the table, help clothe and care for the children and lay warm in their beds at night. This would help them to escape the poorhouse which was a palpable threat looming over all the women.

Datchworth was not known for its empathy for those, who in the minds of its people, 'got what they deserved.' The women would have to fight together for their survival, and support each other, to avoid the worst happening to any of them.

The Shadbolts, a strong and resilient family, were led by no-nonsense men who laboured hard and did their best for one another. They had worked the land for generations, understanding the cycles of nature and the whims of the absent landlords who were interested in profit, not people. But there was a sense of helplessness these days when modern machinery was stealing men's jobs, like a river relentlessly changing the course of history.

The brothers and their uncle had one by one been replaced by machines purchased by the landowners to cut costs. The family was aware of how machines had already stolen jobs in the mines then later the mills.

Sixty years ago workers like themselves had railed against James Watt when he tried to sell the steam engine to the corn millers. Watt had argued that such labour saving devices would win the day in the same way as water mills had replaced grinding the grain by hand.

Watt's was a difficult battle but eventually his prediction proved correct. Now ploughing and reaping was done by machine and land workers were being forced off the land, moving to the towns and cities to seek work that did not exist.

Those with no other choice became railway navvies moving from job to job with their families, living and working in appalling conditions. Women and children were housed in cramped timber or turf huts along the railway tracks, where the men were rough and the settlements were noisy and unruly.

The work was dangerous and did not provide workers' compensation for men who were injured or killed, a not-infrequent occurrence. 'Railway mania,' as it was called, rewarded the investors well but little was paid to the labourers.

There were more men employed on building the railways than serving in the army and the navy put together. Many had poured in from Ireland, and from Europe, where food was scarce for those who were poor; men with little or no choice if they were to feed their own.

So it was that desperate men were pushed to do desperate things: stealing food for wives and children, and cloth for clothes to keep them warm in the cold of winter.

The cruelty of sending these men away was unrecognised by those who had not suffered from hunger or cold, the conscience of the town numbed to the needs of those not as fortunate as themselves.

Chapter 2

Master May, Captain of the *Mayda*, was a confident man who liked to run a tight ship. With the help of his experienced surgeon, Alex Kilroy, he expected to get both convicts and guards to their destination in good health.

The ship's prison was on the lower decks, and spacious enough, with adequate ventilation and light - a far cry from earlier years when men were herded into poorly ventilated cells, left in shackles and lashed for minor misdemeanours.

The mid-deck had tables and chairs set up as a dining area and a place to dry out bedding in rough weather. A space in the bow, referred to as 'the box', served as a deterrent for troublemakers, who could neither lie down nor stand, making it somewhere to be avoided when the sea was rough.

The improved transportation meant more prisoners survived, but the journey was still long and dangerous for all those aboard.

The surgeon was quick to sum up the convicts in his care. They would remain shackled until the ship was underway because a few were hardened criminals who he would need to keep his eye on.

Most were ordinary men ranging in age and circumstance; many were strong, single men who would be useful to the government after they had served their sentence in the colonies. More than half of them could read and write; one in five could read and about the same number were illiterate.

The crimes they had committed, in nearly all cases, were non-violent thefts of food and clothing. Some were army men who had defected or hit an officer in a bout of rage. Others had committed upper-class crimes such as embezzlement or forgery.

Kilroy knew there were men boarding the ship who felt betrayed and were angry at the injustice of courts that treated working men so harshly. Judges showed no consideration for the impact industrialisation had on the men's ability to support their families.

All those aboard would be homesick for the loved ones left behind and village life; fearful, because they had lost control of their lives. These men were not a risk to anyone unless goaded into retaliation.

A few of the men were only too pleased to escape problems in their homeland, especially those with nagging wives or girlfriends who had fallen pregnant. Such men were looking forward to a new beginning.

Kilroy had observed the two oldest men who came aboard the ship. They seemed healthy and capable, and talked earnestly together, planning, perhaps, to bring some leadership to the group.

One was a refined gentleman named Robert Kenyon who had once been a mayor and magistrate. A gentle man, full of kindness, harshly sentenced for the crime of forgery committed to help his fellow man. When the prisoners boarded the ship Kilroy had seen a deputation of concerned citizens gather dockside with a petition asking for mitigation of Kenyon's sentence. Many people who had benefitted from the magistrate's kindness signed the petition but their efforts were ignored.

The other man was Solomon, the oldest of four from the Shadbolt family, all sentenced for stealing food, fabric and clothing from a village store. None, Kilroy noticed, had any prior convictions. He made a mental note: of those boarding the ship today, it was these five married men who should not be leaving wives and children to sail away from England's shores.

Most of the convicts had not been on a boat before; in some cases they hadn't even visited the seaside. So when the ship set sail on a fine August day with little wind in her sails it was a good time for the men to gain their sea-legs. Even in the smooth water some suffered motion sickness, standing by the ship's rails with faces as pale as a wax candle.

When the wind lifted and caught the mainsail the ship began to plane. Water churned and frothed at the stern and soon there were many more heads hanging over the side. The retching and vomiting made some consider jumping overboard to end their suffering.

As the land slipped away the men crowded on deck to watch their homeland dwindle and disappear into the dark blue ocean. None spoke out, not even the guards, when a harmless-looking Irish prisoner pulled a mouth organ from his pocket, put it to his lips and played the sad and haunting melody of the *Londonderry Air*.

Memories flooded the men's minds and emotions were stirred, but not one man moved until the music ended and nothing was left but the sounds of the sea and the wind in the sails. Back in present time, men knew this moment marked the beginning of a life that would change them, some for the better, and some for the worse.

Solomon Shadbolt was fifty years old, with a whiskered face and skin darkened by the sun. He stood five foot four in height. He was tattooed with a picture of a woman on his lower right arm, and on his left a man and a boy. He took his kin George, Ben and

John aside, and told them there was only one way to pay tribute to the families they were leaving behind and that was to concentrate on survival. And, he said, they would do it better than most because they had each other.

"We will deal with one thing at a time, watch each other's back and one day we may be lucky enough to know the story of our children, even if we can never more be a part of their lives."

Solomon and his wife Eleanor had six children, the youngest only three years old. Their oldest daughter, Jemima, had surprised them by running away to London and marrying their nephew, John. John, aged twenty-seven, was clean-shaven with grey eyes, a bright cheerful young man who had loved Jemima, his spirited cousin, for as long as he could remember. Jemima delivered their first child, Martha, in July, while John was locked away in Milbank Prison for his part in the burglary.

Solomon's son George was half his father's age and whiskered like his father. At five foot seven, he was tall for those days. He had a daughter, Julie, eighteen months old, and another baby – to be named George or Georgina – due this month. George was aware he might never see his baby, and his heart ached because he knew his toddler would not remember him. He was a man who took his responsibilities seriously and he feared for his wife, Harriet, who would have to look after two children without his help.

John's brother Ben, who completed the family, was, at a little over twenty years of age, a nuggety five foot five and a half, with a smooth face and blues eyes that twinkled with mischief. His wife, Carolyn, was due to deliver in November, so Clara or Linden was not yet born. How could a family so fragmented in these days of depression survive? What court of law would allow such a thing?

The routine on board ship brought some relief from the long miserable days for both the prisoners and their guards. The surgeon believed in keeping men busy and making sure they took care of hygiene to maintain their health.

The convicts were called to muster on deck at five-thirty in the morning. They carried their bedroll with them and laid it out to air. Half of the convicts at a time would strip off to wash, buffeted by the wind blowing cold across the deck. The washing water was cold, so breakfast time was welcomed as a means of getting warm before returning to the deck if weather permitted.

Every day two men were on duty to clean the mess and the prison, a not-unwelcome chore that brought a change from the normal routine. Dinner was at twelve midday along with a serving of wine or lime juice to prevent scurvy. In the tropics, the lime was increased to a double serving every second day.

Compulsory religious studies followed, designed to help them see the error of their ways. For some this was a comfort; others delighted in rebelling against the hypocrisy. The two factions caused bad feelings to spill over when the men returned to the deck after the meetings, some of them swearing under their breaths and blaspheming.

"We have had enough moralising from men who are no better that us, except they had more luck and the favour of God on their side. Who among them have toiled in harsh conditions under harsher bosses and still gone to bed hungry at night?"

George did find comfort in the words and prayers, and there was religious literature to read to cope with the boredom.

His family helped to keep the peace, with both Solomon and Robert Kenyon acting as a buffer between prisoners intent on stirring up trouble. They settled them down, reminding them the punishment would be 'the box'. Some days they were relieved when it was time to go below, so they could escape the bickering. They often found work with those who were named as cooks for the day and took a share in preparing the evening meal.

After supper they went back on deck until six, a last

chance to breathe the fresh air and spend some time in contemplation before they carried their bedrolls below. Once again they were crowded among men who stifled tears of regret and shouted out during the fearful dreams that haunted them. And so another night would pass and the morning would bring the same routine.

Not until they were nearly six weeks away from the homeland was the routine all but dispensed with. Many of the convicts became sick with diarrhoea and fever. Confined to the stuffy prison deck, they moaned and called out in their sleep with night sweats. The smell of illness below was overwhelming. Those with weak stomachs began a new round of vomiting; the foul liquid sloshed along the floor by the swell of the ocean.

Solomon kept his family close beside him and on deck as much as possible, away from those who were unwell. Robert Kenyon stayed with them and they filled their time with talk of home and the reason they were in this predicament. Robert related how he had fought for a client seeking fair compensation, which had been refused.

Robert falsified documents and when this was discovered there was nothing to be done but face the charges against him. He did not expect to be sent to a colony for hardened criminals. He told how grateful he felt that so many people had put in a good word for him, and how even though he had striven always to be kind and charitable, the judge saw fit to make an example of him and let the decision stand.

Solomon had a story to tell as well, which he felt he could share with this unfortunate man he now counted as a friend.

"There was a murder," he whispered, "five years ago – a man I drank with at the Horns public house at Bulls Green. We both left for home at the same time, a reasonable hour it was and all, but..." he paused for effect, "Tom did not reach his home. The Hertford paper was keen to get plenty of value from the story so they linked the missing man to a murder that took place one year earlier. A reporter wrote a piece reminding everyone about a mutilated body that had been hidden in the moat."

"The police were excited to think they could find a double murderer in the village. I was called to the police station where, I admit, I wasn't forthcoming as a witness, though I made it clear I knew nothing that would help their investigation."

Solomon took his time to continue building to the climax of his story.

"I say to you, in confidence, I believe we have been unfairly sentenced for our crime of burglary and that has much to do with dejected policemen who needed to bolster their crime statistics."

A further pause.

"The truth came out, you see, some days later. Tom was found. He had no wounds and it was evident that he had slipped, fallen into the pond and drowned. There were no suspicious circumstances, a fact that did not seem to have much impact on an over-zealous police force only too happy when the opportunity arose to exaggerate our hapless crime and see us sent away for revenge!"

Robert could find no reason to disagree with his new friend. They had both been hard done by; Solomon even more so, because his entire family had suffered.

The sting of death was soon to visit the ship, the word spreading quickly among the convicts that one of their number had passed.

Due to the hot conditions the man's funeral would be held that very day. Solomon's son and his nephews were shaken, lying awake at night listening to the laboured breathing of men who days ago had been fit and well. In vain they tried to ignore the rank odours of vomit and faeces from men so weakened they seemed not to know or care. And from this death trap there was no escape.

The illnesses had begun early in October, soon after they reached the south-east trade winds. The surgeon blamed the water which had been taken aboard from the River Thames. The filtration was coarse, allowing microbes to slip through and making it unsuitable to be taken on board a ship unable to pick up fresh supplies for months.

By Kilroy's own admission the water had a 'nauseous and astringent taste,' due, he believed, to the oak casks in which it was stored.

From the early nineteenth century, there were many sewer outlets flowing directly into the river Thames with a resultant risk to health. A minimal effort was made to improve this dangerous situation, but by 1845 the threat had been forgotten and things were left to accelerate. It was not until the early 1850s that the tardiness ended in an outbreak of cholera and it was to be another twenty years before a proper system was put in place.

Giant steam driven pumps were built to take the sewerage from the underground pipes up to the surface where it was pumped further along the Thames nearer to the ocean so that it would be flushed out to sea twice a day by the tide.

The ship still had a month to sail before fresh water could be picked up at the Cape of Good Hope around early November.

The prisoners became unsettled after watching their fellow shipmate slipped unceremoniously over the side to a watery grave. Extra prayer meetings had been arranged for those who wanted to pray for both the sick and the healthy, but nothing stopped the spread of disease. A greater number of prisoners were affected, along with crew members and passengers.

Three more prisoners died and were quickly dispatched over the side into the dark and foreboding water, leaving behind an emptiness and uncertainty that was difficult to rise above.

At last the ship arrived at the Cape of Good Hope where they picked up meat and vegetables along with medical supplies and uncontaminated water. To view land again was a relief, and all aboard were on deck for the spectacular sight of Table Mountain, dressed in purple with deeper shadows, set against a sky that appeared to be painted on an artist's canvas awash with colours from azure to pale turquoise. Spirits were lifted, but all too soon the long journey was resumed.

There were to be two other fatalities after the ship left the Cape, though they now had fresh water and food on board. A lance-corporal's wife, her baby almost due, succumbed to a bout of diarrhoea that brought on an early labour. Even the toughest of the convicts felt the anguish as they listened to the woman, weak and listless, wail with the effort of trying to push out the precious life inside her.

The boy child was born, his skin blue, his body lifeless, and his mother held him close to her breast and struggled to stay alive herself. The battle was too great; she did not have the strength and took her last resentful breath the next day.

The sight of a mother, her babe a swaddled bundle beside her, slipping into the ocean triggered despair aboard the ship.

Her death was a reminder to the Shadbolts of those left behind to struggle on their own. This was especially so for Ben; whose own baby was due about this time.

Would his wife Carolyn deliver their baby safely? Would the baby be a girl or a boy? Had she been able to eat enough wholesome food to give her the strength she needed?

Everyone was subdued and in dread of what the next weeks on the sea would bring.

Chapter 3

Edward heard news of Ben Shadbolt's wife, Carolyn, because she had made a plea in the court for her husband's property to be returned to her.

Her request was denied. The goods, she was told, had been confiscated and nothing could be done to recover them. He read in the newspaper that she had borne a baby girl in November, whom she had named Clara.

Carolyn was everything Edward wanted in a woman. She had been out of his reach not only because she was married, but because she was poor.

Yet Carolyn was the kind of woman who stood tall no matter that her clothes were plain, the fabric faded with age, or that her shoes were worn. Carolyn hand-stitched her own dresses. If the fabric lacked colour, the cut suited her figure, showing glimpses of her bosom under the delicate shawls she favoured.

Her natural uncomplicated beauty shone for all to

see. No fashionable styles for her hair that fell like a mane down her back, the colour as rich as golden honey.

On Sundays she plaited it into strands coiled and fastened neat and tight around her head, allowing a sight of the gentle curve of her neck, flowing down to merge with the swell of her bosom.

Edward longed to see her in the expensive clothes he could afford to buy, dresses trimmed with lace and in hues and colours to show off the electric-blue of her eyes.

Solomon's wife, Eleanor, was to demonstrate the strength and stability the younger wives needed after their men were sent away. Eleanor was a midwife and she delivered the three new babies as they became due.

She helped the young women stand up to the humiliation too many of the villagers put them through after the trial.

The winter had been cold and lean, with no men to bring home the pay and so many young ones to care for.

Edward knew in his heart he must find a way to make Carolyn's life easier. He could not stand by and watch as she struggled to work and look after her baby. He knew his own family would be outraged if they realised what he was planning.

Others in the village would be suspicious, too, but he would repeat the words of the minister: 'Do unto others what you would have them do unto you.'

He resolved to begin by ordering the court to return the Shadbolts' property. Though legally this was outside of his jurisdiction, he believed it was important to all the women to have their husbands' things returned.

Edward didn't consider himself a courageous man. Intelligent, dutiful and organised - yes, he was all these things - but unwilling, until now, to put his own position at risk.

Today was different and he entered the Hertford Assizes with his back as straight as a soldier's on parade, and a determination to get what he came for.

"The Shadbolt property."

He spoke deliberately in a tone that brooked no nonsense, but before he could say any more the clerk, who had just dipped his quill in the ink to continue writing a report, waved his arm towards a door.

"All property is in alphabetical order," he said. "Nothing of value left in that lot."

The bag that had Shadbolt written on it was large but manageable so Edward picked it up and walked out. The clerk did not even look up from his desk and

Edward doubted he would even remember who'd been there, and it was unlikely the bag would be missed.

After all, the men who had once owned it were hard at work in the colony by now. Edward looked forward to delivering the prize to Carolyn and her family, and was pleased when an unexpected opportunity came to return the Shadbolt property.

The Cole family felt duty bound to help with the church stall at the village fete each year. Clothes, shoes, tools and kitchenware were collected and stored until the day of the fete. Edward's appointed task was to pick up vegetables and fruit from those with gardens, then deliver them to his mother who was in charge of the produce stall.

Morning dawned with an unclouded blue sky and only the slightest breeze. On such a day everyone would be out, wandering among the stalls to pick up bargains and join in the games set up to amuse the children.

Edward saw Carolyn as soon as she arrived, walking with the women of her family who were surrounded by their small children. Carolyn carried her baby Clara, wrapped in a shawl. He watched as she sorted through the goods on display, picking up clothes with her spare hand and eyeing them for size then putting them down.

The family stopped to watch the village children apple ducking, laughing and chatting as heads bobbed down eagerly into a tank of water trying to catch an apple with their teeth.

Finally, Carolyn walked towards the produce stall where Edward began to rearrange vegetables unnecessarily in an effort to appear useful so that he might get an opportunity to speak with Carolyn.

His fussing irritated his mother.

"Thank you, Edward. I can manage now."

With no excuse to stay longer, he started to move away. Then he noticed Carolyn and her sisters-in-law were buying more than they could possibly carry home. It was easy for a good, church-going man to offer to drop the fruit and vegetables around for them later.

"I would be most grateful, Mr Cole."

As always when Carolyn spoke her words seemed to harmonise with Edward's soul. She smiled.

"We do seem to have bought more than we can carry, the prices are so tempting. We won't be home immediately. Would three this afternoon suit you?"

Edward nodded, relieved things had gone his way with so little effort.

"That will be fine, Mrs Shadbolt. Enjoy your day and can I recommend the free pony rides for the older children."

Edward bid goodbye to Carolyn and her family then picked up the fruit and vegetables and carried them to his horse and gig. He went home, to collect the bag marked Shadbolt and waited until three o'clock.

Edward expected he would need to explain how he had retrieved the bag from the court, but when he arrived at Carolyn's house he found her waiting at the gate with the other women. They took the produce from him, and left Carolyn to convey her thanks.

Carolyn took the bag straight away. She pulled at the strings that held it closed and saw inside the things that were so precious to her. Instead of asking for any explanation she merely bowed her head to hide the tears running down her face and held up her hand to stop him from saying any more.

"You have done a good thing today, Mr Cole. I am in debt to you."

With that she turned towards the gate and carried the bag into her home.

Edward's passion for Carolyn welled up; he could not utter another word. Enough for now that he had made a difference in her life. He had done something worthwhile and that gave him hope. He knew better than to make too much of Carolyn's words and grateful there were no questions to answer, only an unusual trust that things were as they were meant to be.

Carolyn showed the bag to Eleanor, Harriet and Jemima who picked out and clung to clothing that belonged to their husbands, holding individual garments to their faces as a balm to heal their loss. They asked how Edward could have got the bag from the court, when they had been denied and, more importantly, why he had delivered the property back to the family.

"It's a mystery," Carolyn agreed, "and one I will get to the bottom of one day. For now, I'm only pleased and grateful for its return!"

The past eight months since their husbands had been taken away saw them subjected to a certain amount of ridicule and a great deal of hardship, so the women had decided it was best if they all moved into Eleanor's house.

This meant they had little space or privacy, but they could afford to heat one room to keep them warm. They could look after each other's children so that a woman could accept any work that came her way, sharing the wages between them.

The village men were suspicious of the women, afraid to give them work, thinking the women to be thieves like their husbands. This, however, did not stop them making crude and unwanted suggestions to the young women, who may, in their desperation, be taken advantage of. The village women were kinder, knowing Eleanor to be an experienced midwife who they might need to call on one day and therefore more willing to break down the barriers.

The Shadbolt women could learn nothing of what had happened to their men after they sailed. They had been told the ship would take five months to reach Norfolk Island and tales were spreading about the atrocious conditions aboard the convict ships.

Accounts about the weather were troubling too; how it could change from one day to the next and take a vessel to the bottom of the ocean. The women knew, in all likelihood, that some of the men might not reach their destination. They grieved their loss, be it to the sea, illness or the fifteen years to be served in this 'hell hole of the Pacific.'

They stood tall and took a pride in raising their babies, and felt some comfort as the little ones grew and began to reflect a likeness to their fathers. A sense of continuity prevailed that lessened somewhat the pain of separation.

Unlike the other wives, Carolyn had not been born in Datchworth so she relied heavily on Ben's family. She had met the Shadbolts through Ben's brother, Peter, who worked on a farm near her hometown.

Peter had invited her to join them for his wife's

birthday, and the family that arrived for the celebration included Ben.

The attraction was immediate and mutual. Ben was more outgoing than his brother, and had moved from job to job, learning as he went. A strong and thickset man, his shock of dark hair framed a square, determined face. His carefree nature, the joy he found in living, drew Carolyn to him.

He was someone she could look up to and she believed he would make something of himself.

Carolyn was an accomplished horse rider and soon learned that Ben knew more about horses than anyone she'd met, and was well-known around the district as able to pick a good horse from a mile away.

They began courting from that day, meeting at Peter's house whenever Ben could travel to see her, and riding the farm horses over the hills together.

When Peter changed his job to be closer to Datchworth and nearer his family, Ben and Carolyn knew it was time for them to settle down together. Soon the banns were read and they became man and wife.

Carolyn was eighteen years old.

Chapter 4

On board the *Mayda*, the dying ended. The ship sailed through some easier weather conditions, bringing a level of peace. A sense of well-being was felt by all aboard including the soldiers guarding the prisoners.

These guards were in many ways as much victims of the times as those they were guarding.

Food shortages throughout the British Isles and Europe drove men to seek work that offered the security they sought and regular pay, enabling them to help support their families by sending money home.

When the orders came to travel across the world as guards on a convict ship, it had seemed like a welcome change.

In reality, it was not what they expected. The soldiers saw men who had been in similar circumstances to themselves, without work and hungry, driven to break the law. Now these young men were being transported to act as servants of the

Crown, sent to set up colonies for queen and country.

Conversation between the convicts and the guards was not allowed beyond the necessary, but it was easy for the soldiers to pick out the regular criminals from the unfortunate workers who had fallen on hard times.

By early January the long journey was almost over, but not without a setback. This time it was the weather rather than putrid water and illness that proved to be the enemy. During the night a storm crossed their path and pushed the ship and its passengers to the limit.

The vessel rolled and crashed through waves that sent water washing over the decks with such fury that the deckhands had to be tied to the mast or rails. The ship lurched and shuddered as it climbed up the waves then slid down the other side, sending anything that was not secured skidding across the cabin.

The noise was strident, rasping and discordant and, when it mixed with the howling of the wind, one could easily believe a chasm would open and swallow the ship and all aboard. Even the toughest of the prisoners called out for the misery to end as nausea returned and dizziness overtook them.

"Let her sink!" they cried, while other men knelt in prayer, propped up as best they could to make a bargain with the god they had earlier rejected. The crack of the foremast mast breaking led them to believe their plea had been heard, but the ship rolled and bucked even more.

Captain and crew held the ship's head to the wind and spurred her on until the dawn, when the wind subsided and it was over. All hands were on deck to repair the damage and a few trusted convicts who managed to keep their feet helped to clear the debris.

At last they came within sight of land, in the distance at first but coming closer and closer until the Union Jack could be seen flying over Kingston, reviving memories of home. But this land was not home, and did not resemble England in the least. The trees grew straight and strong, shaped like a pyramid. The trunks that seemed at first as if they'd make good masts to replace those broken at sea were full of knots and could serve no such purpose.

Norfolk Island lay five hundred miles north of New Zealand and was nearly one thousand miles in distance from Australia. The many rocky cliffs and shores around the island were prone to choppy seas, making safe landing of the boats difficult. The few sandy beaches were blocked by coral reefs over which only small craft could sail.

It had been visited in early days by Polynesian voyagers who, apart from leaving clues behind such as adzes and banana trees, had decided this was not to be home, moving on where there was easier access or perhaps sensing the disturbing future the Island was to encounter.

The *Mayda* anchored in the clear blue waters off the bay. Each prisoner was checked by the surgeon to make sure he was fit to work. Though most passed, a few were sent to the hospital because they had not yet recovered from the sickness the putrid water had brought upon them.

The prisoners were transferred to a whale boat, crammed uncomfortably close to each other, and transported to the jetty. They set foot on land for the first time in five months, relieved at the prospect of solid earth under their feet. Instead, at each step forward they lurched unsteadily like drunks. Some had to stop to vomit before being forced to continue.

The walk to the prison buildings though not far was uphill, affording no respite, and they could expect little sympathy from the guards who yelled and prodded them on with their muskets.

"Keep moving, you landlubbers. We aren't got all day."

The men were brought to a halt in front of the main prison, built of stone, cold and forbidding even from the outside. A whipping post was visible through the gates. No grass grew on the surrounding ground and the bare dirt, dark in colour, was packed hard and crusted with the blood of men punished by the biting lash of the whip.

The prisoners were quickly sorted into groups depending on their skills and instructed as to where they would sleep for the first night.

The four Shadbolt men were known to be agricultural labourers and were selected with others to form a group responsible for growing food to sustain the inhabitants; more particularly, for the families of the administrators who lived in modern houses further up the hill above the prison.

Captain May and Dr Kilroy walked past the prisoners to comfortable accommodation at such a house, where they would rest on land for a few nights until they received new orders. It wasn't long before both men realised they had brought their passengers to a place where change was urgently required.

The surgeon, understanding the basic needs of men, hoped such change would happen sooner rather than later.

The first night on shore was to set the pattern for what the future held for the one hundred and ninety-four who had survived the voyage on the *Mayda*. The prison cells allowed barely enough room to sleep either four or eight men. The new prisoners watched in dismay as the weaker and younger men who had journeyed with them were keenly eyed by the older, hard-faced men who had preceded them to the island.

The guards turned their backs at lock-up, refusing to acknowledge how the old hands attempted to nudge some of the newcomers by force away from their allotted cells. Most were quick to free themselves and move closer to their shipmates.

Others were not so lucky and were now at risk, subject to abuse, treated as slaves and used for sexual gratification. The guards remained oblivious to any cries for help.

The Shadbolts – by God's miracle, George believed – were assigned the same room. So they had a certain amount of privacy and time to prepare for what they now knew would be a battle, not only with the establishment, but with prison gangs.

Breakfast was dished up early, a coarse maize meal, ground by hand, which none of the newcomers were used to eating. Before long, the less hardy amongst them were ill again with diarrhoea.

The surgeon was saddened by how quickly men he had taken care of on the journey were ending up in hospital. He thought to intervene, but his advice to wean them on to the maize meal slowly fell on deaf ears. He could do no more. The *Mayda* was due to sail, and the last link the transportees had with their homeland would soon be gone.

After the ship departed, the men chosen to work

on the land were taken to Cascade Station on the northern, more sheltered side of the island. Here the land was fertile and suited the chosen crops. The huts here were of wood instead of the stone buildings in Kingston with sleeping bunks for up to twenty men in each, and a mess area. The huts were set out to form a square that gave added protection.

A cookhouse, an old building used as a chapel, and the chaplain's residence completed the station. There was no jail as such, but a few cells, small and poorly ventilated, had been built for solitary confinement.

The work in the fields was the most hated because the drudgery was constant. Men in chains were sent to labour from dawn to dusk no matter the season or the weather. The ground was hard and there were to be no ploughs for the men to use. Digging was done by hand, with rows of men toiling when a plough would have broken the soil with ease.

Solomon and his son and nephews were relieved to be away from the conditions they had seen in Kingston on their arrival. Working the fields at least produced results, even though they did not get to eat much of the food they tended.

There was no hospital in Cascades. A convict was in charge of dispensing drugs, a pale undernourished fellow, who knew nothing of hygiene as was evident by the dirt under his fingernails.

As fate would have it, the man became poorly himself and was taken to the hospital at Kingston. The next day Solomon's friend Robert Kenyon was brought to Cascades to take over the dispensary along with clerical duties.

This, then, was what the next fifteen years would be like for the Shadbolts, toiling in chains for long days and watched over by ex-convicts and corrupt supervisors.

Sleep was slow coming at night because normal movement during the day caused the shackles to bite into their ankles, leading to wounds that throbbed and kept them awake, reminding them of what the next day would bring. They talked of home and wondered about the babies they had left behind to be raised without a father, or by the hand of another.

They thought about their womenfolk. The men tried not to let their thoughts wander to the intimacy they had shared with their wives; the pain was too great to bear. To allow such indulgence would not improve their chances of survival. There could be life after this hell if they managed to keep their minds on the future, and not dwell on the past. Instead they had to listen to the rustle of bedding and the moans of men seeking relief from yearnings that could not otherwise be satisfied in this cruel and unnatural incarceration.

Each man had his own methods of dealing with his pain. Solomon became the patriarch and was like a second father to his nephews. He was much younger than his brother Benjamin and the boys spent much of their time with him and their cousins. Solomon knew he had to be an example to the younger men and he took his responsibility seriously.

At home in Datchworth, his wife Eleanor was playing a similar role, taking the young wives under her wing. Their son George missed his little girl and craved to greet and know the baby born after he left. A rational man, he found solace in the chapel and was content to spend time in prayer and in taking guidance from the chaplain.

The brothers Ben and John used the work they did, and their love of the land to give them strength and the will to carry on. Ben was known by his family to be feisty so they kept a close eye on him.

The temptation to argue and fight back when things got tough with supervisors and troublesome roommates was difficult for them all, but the consequences were to be avoided. Time in solitary confinement could pull a man down quickly and the family knew they had to stay strong if they wanted to survive.

Other men complained about how tough the work was and spent much of their time finding excuses to stay out of the fields, faking illness or injuring themselves. This served only to add to their problems. Solitary confinement might play on the mind and soul, but to be sent back to Kingston, and end up under the influence of the gangs, was to be even worse off.

The six months that followed the arrival of the *Mayda* brought major changes to the Island, and not for the better. Things became so much worse that they heralded a depth of fear and loathing not previously experienced.

The Shadbolt men had seen for themselves that Kingston was not a good place to be imprisoned, and were pleased to have been taken to the Cascades, away from the gangs.

They learned from the older prisoners already there how the previous commander, Captain Maconochie, had given the prisoners their own plots to tend, and utensils to cook their own food. He had set up a points system that offered the men a certain dignity, and an opportunity to earn rewards as well as encouraging rehabilitation.

Over time the current administrator, Major Joseph

Childs, who had been in charge for nearly two years, withdrew the privileges that had allowed for a measure of contentment.

By July of 1846, the prisoners became even more unsettled because Childs had lengthened the hours of work, leaving no time for private farm plots. He cut prisoners' rations and withdrew rest days earned for good behaviour.

These decisions were foolish enough, but what followed was to start a riot known as the cookhouse mutiny.

Even though Major Childs was about to be replaced as the administrator, he pushed the prisoners one step too far. On the 1st of July he decreed that the prisoners would eat only what was served from the kitchen. All cooking equipment was to be handed in.

The news was too much for the prisoner known as 'Jacky-Jacky,' a former bushranger who had escaped the death sentence two years earlier in Australia. Lawrence Kavanagh was known for his gentlemanly ways and dubbed Jacky-Jacky by the Aborigines. Governor Sir John Eardley had seen the good in the prisoner and had commuted his sentence.

Now this young man could suffer the cruelty of oppression no longer; he would lead a revolt. He warned, "any that join me will swing from the Major's gallows."

His followers were unafraid of the gallows; men who would rather die than live like animals chained to the wheel of the crank mill with ninety-nine others, grinding maize into flour. Any man punished by forced labour at the mill knew the effort it took to turn the wheel that kept the grinder moving. The work was so arduous that those listening to the men could believe they were listening to 'the cries of lost souls.'

The revolt was carried out in a rage pent up for too long. Four officials were clubbed to death with axes and farm tools. Though they begged for their lives for the sake of their families, the convicts could find no pity in their hearts. Soldiers with muskets moved in and managed to persuade the convicts to withdraw. Their fury quelled, the men laid down their weapons.

Major Childs had no stomach for dealing with the men he had pushed to such violence. He was pleased to be able to hand that over to the new administrator, John Giles Price. Price organised the trial, found seventeen men guilty and sentenced them to death.

Nor did he stop there. A strong deterrent was required and he ordered every prisoner on the Island to be brought to watch as first twelve and then five more men were hung by the neck until dead.

The Shadbolts stood where they had first gathered on this godforsaken island, and now there was the chilling presence of the gallows beside the prison entrance. The whipping post was stained now; men had recently been flogged. The blood flowed down their backs and then trickled onto to the ground. Where salt water had been thrown over wounds, pools of slush remained underfoot.

Why had they been lashed? For asking for more food, perhaps, or for faking illness; or for being caught with tobacco, sometimes planted on them by others as a form of revenge.

The new commander, John Giles Price, assured those who would question him that he had an aversion to flogging; however, he still believed it was a necessary means of enforcing obedience of the regulations.

Thus began a regime of terror that was unrecognised far too long by those of higher authority.

The Shadbolt men faced the gallows to show respect for their fellow prisoners, watching as one by one the condemned walked up the steps towards the noose that hung against its own shadow on the stark prison wall.

The hangman put the rope around each neck and pulled it tight, though not so tight as to restrict the breath. The drop was too short to break the neck and arms and legs jerked out of control as dying men struggled vainly to fill their lungs with air.

The one or two minutes it took for merciful

unconsciousness to precede death seemed to pass in slow motion for the bystanders. For the poor souls on the end of the rope, so callously despatched, it would have seemed much longer.

One man who had survived the ordeal of hanging by the short rope described it.

"The first second lasted for one thousand years, I felt my arms and legs jerking out of control. I was trying to fill my lungs with air, but they were crumpled up like paper bags."

Traumatised prisoners muttered among themselves, some saying those being hung were the lucky ones. Their oppression and pain was over: no more grinding grain, no more slaving in the fields, no more fighting for food, and no struggling to maintain the strength to survive.

Jacky-Jacky, who was twenty-six years of age, was the last to climb the steps. He stood tall and recited the words he had written for the chaplain to pass on to his family.

"Out of the bitter cup of misery, I have drunk from my sixteenth year. The sweetest draft is that which takes away the misery of the living death. It is the friend that deceives no man: all will be quiet; no tyrant will disturb my repose."

Chapter 5

Solomon's older brother Benjamin and his wife Catherine prayed every day to God that He would watch over Solomon, his son George, and their own two boys, John and Ben.

Nothing could fill the void of their absence; this strong faith in God and his protection was the only relief they could find.

Soon Benjamin and Catherine's house became a haven for the wives of their sons and nephew. By the time Ben and Carolyn's Clara was born, the older couple were in the habit of looking after all the Shadbolt babies when the mothers needed a break or an opportunity to seek out work.

1840 might have been a romantic period for some in society, such as the poets, artists and thinkers. True, there was an increasing interest in the arts and politics were more liberal; yet class and gender distinctions were still very much alive.

Women were expected to stay at home and tend to the daily needs of husbands and children. They were treated with disdain if they were forced to work, so opportunities to make money were few and work generally unpleasant and poorly paid whether in factories, hand-stitching clothes and hats, or washing and cleaning for the better off.

Carolyn found the best work was cleaning and washing clothes in the big houses because it didn't entail the long hours in a factory that made it difficult to spend enough time with her daughter Clara. She was often harassed by the man of the house, who thought she could be tempted to exchange her favours for extra money. Refusal could mean the loss of the job but she stayed strong, wanting to keep her good reputation so that she could one day meet a man and remarry.

Sometimes her mind wandered to the memory of how kind Edward Cole had been when he returned Ben's property three months earlier. He was a handsome man, who always treated her as though she was special. He intrigued her. He would allow his eyes to linger on her face, listening to every word when she spoke with him.

If his kindness was based on pity, she didn't mind. Edward Cole made her feel worthy, womanly, at a time when she most needed it.

Most weekends, Edward spent horse-riding with his friend in the country. He had tried to put Carolyn from his mind, but it was at this friend's house that he got the chance to meet her again.

Carolyn's brother-in-law, Peter, was the herdsman for the dairy cows on his friend's property. Peter and his wife Ann had been supportive of all the Shadbolt women, keeping them supplied with milk for the children. Peter felt especially responsible towards Carolyn because he had first introduced her to his brother Ben. On this occasion Carolyn, who was known for her hairdressing skills, had come to repay their generosity by cutting their children's hair.

Late that afternoon when Edward's party returned from their ride, Carolyn was making ready to leave. He watched as she hugged Ann and Peter, then bent to kiss her nieces and nephews.

Edward estimated it was more than an hour's walk for her to get back to the village and the weather was turning cool. He observed what the time was as she set off along the road, then he turned and followed his friends into the house for a drink before he made his own way home.

"Does the Shadbolt woman visit the farm often?" Edward kept his tone casual. "It's a long walk for a woman on her own."

"Regularly, and she enjoys the horses. I've seen her

riding Peter's farm hack. No saddle! She takes the mare for a canter across the fields and back, then spends time brushing her down. She has little to call her own, I reckon, so if it gives her some joy, it can do no harm."

"Indeed, indeed. No harm at all."

A smile played on Edward's lips. He was already plotting how he could take advantage of this discovery.

Carolyn had walked less than half way to the town when Edward caught up with her in his gig. He drove past then pulled over. She approached the gig and gave him a friendly smile.

"Would you like a ride to town, Mrs Shadbolt? It's getting cold and you've got a way to go."

Carolyn ran her hand down the horse's mane then took hold of the bridle. She began to whisper softly to the mare. Her other hand followed the horse's face from its ears to the soft pink nose.

"What's her name?"

"This is Betsy. I've had her since she was a foal."

"She is beautiful. I had a pony as a child. She was a dapple grey like Betsy. I miss her."

"Then would you like to drive her home? You can groom her when we get to my house. I've things to get ready for work tomorrow, so you'd be doing me a favour."

Carolyn stepped lightly up into the gig and, for the first time in his life, Edward knew things were as they should be. The two spoke of their love of horses and how Carolyn enjoyed visiting Peter and Ann on the farm.

"Do you go hunting in season, Mr Cole?" she asked.

"I prefer not to see any animal hurt," he confided. "Even foxes. I usually find an excuse not to go."

Carolyn, laughing, made her own confession.

"When I was a child I would run to my bedroom and cover my head so I couldn't hear the hounds during the hunting season."

The ride home ended too soon for Edward and he spent more time than he needed to showing Carolyn around the stables and explaining where he kept his brushes and horse blankets. At times he was so close to her he could count her eyelashes and smell the sweet scent of thyme in her hair.

Carolyn began to work with Betsy, and was soon so absorbed that Edward thought it best to leave them to it. A bond had been formed between his horse and the woman he admired.

Carolyn arrived home much later than if she had walked, but more alive than she had felt since Ben was taken nearly a year ago.

"I think I could get work grooming and feeding Edward Cole's horse, Betsy, through the winter months," she announced. "It's easy work and something I would enjoy for a change."

"So that's what kept you," exclaimed Harriet. "We were beginning to worry."

"Mr Cole overtook me in his gig when I was on my way home and he offered me a ride. I stayed to brush Betsy down in return for his kindness."

And so it was arranged that Carolyn took over the care of Betsy. She rode the mare along the country roads, allowing her to feed on the grass verges; mucked out her stable and laid hay on the ground. She brushed her until she shone and took care of her saddle and bridle. Edward would join them every Saturday with a generous pay packet for Carolyn.

He found excuses to talk with her about the horse's health and well-being, congratulating Carolyn on her animal husbandry. Each week he lingered longer.

"How is your family getting along?" he would enquire. Then, "Mrs Shadbolt, I brought too much fruit from the market. Will you take some home for the children?"

"Thank you, Mr Cole."

She would accept what he offered and repay him by doing extra jobs – and in ways she wasn't even aware of. Edward appreciated the faith Carolyn showed in him when she began to share things about herself and her emotions; gratified that she felt able to confide in him.

She spoke about Clara and what a good girl she was.

"She keeps growing out of her clothes faster than I can make more for her."

"Is she walking yet?"

"Almost. She can stand on her own and clap her hands at the same time."

They laughed together at such cleverness, and Edward dared to take her hand.

"Clara's father would be proud of you, Carolyn. You have raised his daughter well."

Carolyn lowered her face. Now she was fighting back the tears.

"It's painful not knowing what's happened to him. At least he has his brother and cousin with him, and the uncle he loved so much. I promised Ben I would find a father for Clara. And if he survives, he is free to find someone new."

Edward's heart went out to Carolyn. Gently he lifted her face.

"No one should go through the pain you've been through," was all he needed to say.

Edward was aware of the strict rules regarding divorce enforced by the Anglican Church regarding women. Carolyn would not be able to remarry for seven years. Edward believed the clergy still held far too much power over women, upholding a man's right to take a woman's possessions and treat them as they pleased; even beating your wife would go unpunished.

The Marriage Act of 1836 allowed non-religious marriages to be held in Registry Offices, but made no provision for women to divorce if they were ill-treated or deserted, which would allow them to restart their lives sooner than seven years.

Edward wanted Carolyn to be his forever, but there were major obstacles to overcome, the first and most difficult being the legality of the union. He would be happy to take Carolyn into his home to love and protect, but Carolyn would not allow that unless she was his wife.

Secondly, his parents would not understand him falling in love with the wife of a man transported for burglary. Hurt, they would certainly be; and may even disinherit him. Friends and work colleagues would be equally hard to convince, but he cared little for their opinion.

Carolyn stepped towards Edward and rested her head on his shoulder. When he put his arms around her, she relaxed into his warmth and strength. She was aware how hard it would be to battle on her own for another six years before she was able to legally wed another. It was difficult to leave the safety of Edward's embrace, but Carolyn knew she would have to face the immediate future alone.

She lifted her head and he registered the regret in her eyes as she moved away before the desperation of her situation became too much to bear.

Carolyn walked home with an ache in her heart, letting the tears run freely down her face. She longed for Ben to return and get to know Clara; to make them a proper family, but she knew this could never be. She thought about how calm she was around Edward, how he knew how often she was lonely and worried.

He had allowed her to forget her troubles briefly in his arms, yet he asked nothing from her, allowing a deep trust to build between them.

Chapter 6

The winter at Cascades was difficult for the men working in the fields. The southerly wind blew through their inadequate clothing with a chill hard work could not ease.

The ground was hard and the hoes recoiled in their hands as the men walked the long rows, tilling the soil. The cruel decision not to use ploughs in the fields was to teach the convicts a lesson - hard work was supposed to keep them out of trouble.

The seasons were not what the men were used to. The coldest months fell in June, July and August and they knew families back home would be basking in the warm days of summer, while here they struggled not to yield to the cold.

They worked without leg irons now, and had done so since the winter began. This didn't compensate for the lack of food and proper sustenance. All of them were thin and their health was deteriorating.

Any thought of rebellion against the conditions was tempered by the vivid memories of the hangings a year before.

Ben, George and John Shadbolt had duties other than the fields including caring for the flock of sheep that provided meat for the administrators and their wives and children. Ben killed the sheep, skinned them and hung them in a tree where they would be collected for use in Kingston.

The prisoners who worked in the mess began to murmur about how they could make a fine meal with a leg or shoulder from the carcass if they had the chance.

"We could get through more work with a decent feed in our bellies," they prompted.

"Yes," another prisoner responded, "we owe it to ourselves to do something about that. One sheep wouldn't even be missed".

The cook butted in, frowning. "I don't know about that."

He was a cautious man and didn't want to lose his position in the kitchen.

The men spent many an evening dreaming of a pot of mutton stew. Like most things that begin in the mind as a wistful daydream, it wasn't long before the young men wanted to turn that dream into reality. They got together and hatched a plan to improve their diet.

Ben approached the cook to check if he could expect any help from that quarter, but the man was afraid and wanted nothing to do with the plan. They were on their own.

The next day, while John kept watch, Ben separated a tender hogget from the flock, then went back after dark to slaughter the animal and hang it high in a tree. The following night he cut off a leg and brought it back to the kitchen.

George put it in a pot to simmer and went back to bed for a few hours. It wasn't difficult to hide the meat in the early hours of the morning. They went back each night and brought a quarter of the animal back to cook. The mutton fed twenty men for five nights. Then they waited a month before killing another so as not to raise suspicion.

The betrayal, when it came, was by an ex-convict who had been employed as overseer because he had been around a long time and knew what tricks the men got up to. This bitter old man was spindly in build and known to the cons as 'Spider'. He was always keen to get the rewards and special privileges offered for snitching on the prisoners.

Spider knew something was going on; he could read the signs yet he couldn't quite put his finger on it. Then one night, unable to sleep, he began to snoop around. A faint smell of cooked meat wafted out from the kitchen. Windows had been left open to clear the air, but the pot simmering gently on the stove was all the evidence he needed.

"Keep it quiet, Spider, and we'll cut you in," Ben cajoled the old-timer.

"You're not talkin' me int' breakin' the rules," Spider retaliated. "You'll all pay dearly for this!"

Spider exited speedily from the barracks before the men could do him harm.

Ben and George were put on trial and given three months hard labour at the mill in Kingston. John was charged with neglect of duty and put back in leg irons. Conditions in Kingston were even worse than the two men had imagined.

There was a hatred among the men, mostly directed at those who refused to bend to the pressure of sexual advances or share their food. Most hated were the prisoners who purposefully hurt themselves so that they would be put in hospital to avoid work. It was easy for those with a grudge to plant tobacco in the men's bunks or clothing, knowing this would be punished by flogging, solitary confinement, or both.

'Solitary' in Kingston was a pit dug deep down into the earth; a dark, damp hole with scarcely any fresh air. Time spent in the pit contributed to the death of many prisoners who were already suffering from insufficient food and proper rest. Severe punishment indeed for crimes they may not even have committed.

The work at the crank mill was tough for Ben and George, even though they were used to the hard work in the fields. Throughout the day it sucked the life out of them, and nights were hell with the torturous abrasions from the shackles and the constant sparring from wretched men who wanted to prove themselves stronger or tougher than the men from the fields.

Each new day brought the familiar sounds from the mill, sounds heard as a discordant sequence. Firstly, the men's feet shuffling round a cumbersome and appallingly heavy wheel. This had to be turned to drive two gigantic stones deployed to grind the maize for use in the kitchen.

Secondly, the clanking of the metal grinding and jangling into action, a noise that could be heard for miles around. There was no escaping the loathsome sound that forecasts the misery of men spurred on by a guard seated on a wall above them.

The guard watched and derided those who did not pull their weight so as to move the wheel at an equal pace, though it was evident all the men were not equal in strength, whether physical or mental.

Later in the day the sound came from the throats of men, rasping, dry and heavy with sorrow.

Ben did not hear the sound from his own lips, but

as he watched his cousin strain forward with mouth open and chin raised, the ligaments taut on neck and shoulders, he knew he himself was contributing to the wails that bounced back off the concrete walls. This was the march of one hundred men that had no end until the day was done.

Solomon tried to find out how his boys were coping in Kingston, but that proved difficult. Now they had committed a crime they were watched more closely. In the end, it was the chaplain who brought news of George, of whom he'd grown fond, passing on a message to Robert when he dropped off a parcel for the dispensary.

The news did not put Solomon's mind at ease. The young men, the chaplain informed him, were suffering at the mill and at the hands of the gangs. The cousins were tough and able to use their fists to defend themselves, but they had chosen not to react to the taunts of the men. They preferred to do their time, stay out of trouble, and get back to Cascade Bay and their kin.

That night Solomon allowed his mind for once to wander back to Datchworth and the family he had left behind. He knew Eleanor was strong and would support the younger women as best she could.

Ben and John's brother Peter had always had a soft spot for Carolyn since he introduced her to Ben. He was a good man and would watch over her. Even though times were hard he would bring milk for the infants when he could.'

"There's a future in commercial dairy farming," Peter had told his uncle. "I'm going to own my own farm one day."

Solomon could not imagine how Peter's hopes and dreams would come true, but he steadfastly prayed for him. In the meantime he was relieved to know that Peter would do what was right by his nieces and nephews.

Tears flowed down Solomon's face, tears of frustration and anger. There was nothing he could do to ease the hardship his family was going through.

"Where will it all end?" he mused. "Will I live to see Datchworth again? Will the women remarry?"

When his tears finally ran dry, Solomon rubbed his eyes and reminded himself he had to be strong and focus on the family he could protect. The close family bond was what would keep this family together, not only in Datchworth but also here in Cascade Bay.

Chapter 7

Clara was turning two years old and Edward had suggested a picnic in the country.

"I have bought a new carriage with room for us all. Betsy needs some exercise so we could drive to the farm to visit Peter and Ann. How would you like that?"

"I would like that just fine, Mr Cole, and I know Clara would be thrilled to ride with Betsy and visit her aunt and uncle."

The three set off early. Carolyn showed Clara how to hold out some grass for Betsy to nibble, then helped her to clamber up onto the fine red quilted seat. Edward put the picnic basket that Mrs Ellis had prepared in the box on the back and then assisted Carolyn to seat herself beside Clara.

Betsy was a fine sight in front of the gleaming new carriage. To those who didn't know better, here was a perfectly happy family going out for the day. Clara chattered in her own language and pointed at cows, birds and horses. Carolyn and Edward had little chance to say more than a few words.

"I am extremely pleased you and Clara were able to come, Carolyn."

"I do feel grand to be travelling in such style."

When they came to a bridge, Edward pulled Betsy off the road.

"It's sheltered here by the stream. I'll put down the rug on the grass ready for our picnic."

For too long a time Carolyn had done nothing so normal and she couldn't wait to lift Clara down and settle her by the water.

"What a delicious picnic Mrs Ellis has put together."

Carolyn chose an egg sandwich for Clara, then poured cider for Edward.

"I'll have some of that pigeon pie, please; it looks delicious."

He smiled as he cut her a generous slice.

"Nothing but the best for my girls today."

Carolyn wasn't sure how to respond to this comment. She leaned over to wipe Clara's chin, which didn't need it, to save herself from replying.

"We'll keep the birthday cake until afternoon tea at Peter and Ann's house, shall we?" suggested Edward.

Carolyn agreed and began to pack away the uneaten food. Edward took Clara down to the stream.

She laughed out loud when he tipped her upside down so she could trail her hands in the rippling water.

Much was made of cutting the cake at Peter's house, where Clara was greeted with hugs and comments on how big she had grown. The children took their cake outside to eat, and the grown-ups smiled at the sight of Clara playing with her cousins. She ran around, imitating the moos of the cow and the quacks of the ducks. The chickens pecked around her feet for cake crumbs.

The men talked about farming and the state of England and Europe while the women talked about the children, and watched them play until they wore themselves out. Peter was first to notice Clara was tiring.

"I've got a birthday present for you, Clara. Come and see."

He hoisted her onto his shoulders and carried her out to the cowshed. Carolyn followed. On a sack was a mother cat with five kittens snuggled beside her. When they heard voices, they stretched out legs and arched backs and tumbled over each other.

Peter set Clara down to study the kittens. Carolyn showed her how to hold one, and Clara picked up each kitten one by one, until she finally held on to a ball of fluff with a white face and tail.

Carolyn laughed. "I think she's chosen the one she

wants."

The trip home gave Edward and Carolyn time to talk. Clara had curled up with her kitten, pulled the rug up over herself and fallen asleep. Edward began to talk, for the first time, about how his wife and child had died.

"Our daughter Anne would have been three years old in a few weeks," he said. "Clara has filled that gap, Carolyn. I would like to see her more often, with your permission."

"I think that would be fine." She paused. "Do you think the kitten could sleep in Betsy's stable? We don't have much space at our house. Would you mind?"

"Perfect. We'll train her to keep the mice down."

Edward's heart pounded so loudly in his chest he feared Carolyn would hear it. He had not dared to believe things would work out this well. Carolyn noticed the content on Edward's face and knew she had made a decision that would change her life.

"We'll drop Clara home with her aunties," she said, "and I'll rub Betsy down and make a bed for the kitten."

The animals were soon settled.

"Shall we finish the cider to end a perfect day?" Edward suggested.

Carolyn nodded, smiling. Together they walked into

the spacious front room, whose pure white walls were the perfect backdrop for the tall grandfather clock with its brass pendulum that swung gently to and fro. The chairs, upholstered in taupe and blue-striped linen, were inviting, but Carolyn chose to seat herself on the chaise longue. Round buttons covered with the same blue velveteen pinched the cloth into dimples.

Carolyn's gaze travelled the room, noting the fireplace set ready to light and the gleam of the brass chandelier. The room suited Edward, it could even be said it reflected his nature: a man with a purity of thought and concern for others.

Edward poured the cider and brought the glasses over, setting them down on the round white table beside the couch. Then he sat beside her.

"That, Carolyn, is what I would call a perfect day."

He leant over to kiss her cheek, at the same moment Carolyn turned her face towards him, and whispered, "Indeed, Mr Cole, it was."

Edward set his glass down on the round white table beside the couch then did the same with the one he had handed Carolyn, he took her hands, pulled her to him and kissed her tenderly on the lips. His body responded with such raw desire, he knew he would have to find an excuse to walk away. But Carolyn lifted a hand to his face and drew him towards her.

There was no turning back.

Edward stood up and lifted Carolyn into his arms. He carried her up the wooden staircase that curved gently towards the upper floor. Family photos on the wall came into view then disappeared.

His bedroom was painted cream, not white, contrasting pleasantly with the varnished furniture with its brass handles. The lace curtains were the only feminine touch. Edward lowered her, unresisting, onto the bed that dominated the room.

"I love you, Carolyn. I want to take care of you and Clara. I already think of her as my own."

"I know you will, Edward."

Carolyn reached up and drew him down beside her.

Nothing counted for either of them except this one moment in time.

Chapter 8

Antrim, a village in Ireland, 1845
Catherine ran down the path to meet her three sons, arms outstretched as if to hold them close forever. She knew her enlisted sons Arthur, John and James had been ordered to serve as guards on a convict ship headed for Australia and beyond.

Catherine feared this might be the last time she saw her boys together. She had questions for them to answer, and cold despair in her heart.

The three brothers wrapped their arms around their mother, encircling her in a cocoon of love. Soon the younger children who had heard the commotion ran out to join them, hanging on to the men's legs.

Catherine's daughter-in-law, Esther, watched the family from outside the circle as they hugged and laughed together. She shared the joy that radiated towards her, tinged with regret. The memories of this visit might have to last them for ever.

Arthur, the eldest, was first to step back. He inspected his mother, who looked far too lean and exhausted. When he had last seen her, Catherine had been an attractive, full-figured woman, strong in body from working in the fields, and strong enough in mind to overcome the loss of her husband three years ago.

"How are you managing?" Arthur enquired, with growing concern.

He stared around the farm. The familiar house he hadd grown up in and the old cow yard had both fallen into disrepair. The thatch on the farmhouse was sparse and the walls needed re-plastering.

Catherine sighed.

"We survive, son, is all I can say. Neighbours help when they can but everyone is suffering."

The potato crop had failed the year before and now the blight that had ravaged Europe had come to Ireland. The potatoes were rotting in the field, the stench a constant reminder of the troubles ahead. And Catherine would have to deal with the savage reality of food shortages entirely on her own.

The young men knew Ireland was not safe these days, overrun as it was by men who were out of work and had taken to thieving to survive; they visited farms after dark taking milk from the house cows and chickens from their coops.

On a still cold night such a gang of thieves came to

the Wallace farm. A heavy dew covered the ground and the moon was but a slice in the sky. Not a night for any honest men to be outdoors. Catherine heard a ruckus near the cow yard, but stayed silent, hoping Will had not heard the sounds. But he was already donning his coat and hat to check what was going on.

"Don't go," Catherine begged. "It could be desperate men come to steal. They will not be inclined to listen to reason."

Will Wallace was taller than most, a stubborn man – tough-minded, he said – and used to looking after what was his. He was physically strong with shoulders and arms that could lift a man on the end of his shovel. This night was different. The gang of men, five in number, were unkempt, uncaring and determined to take what they came for, leaving no clues behind them.

When all was quiet, Catherine ventured out to find Will lying in the yard, his head bloody, and his own kindling axe beside him. Slumped on the ground beside her husband of thirty years, she wept for earlier, kindlier times when there was food in plenty and their little farm was a haven for them and their children.

The Wallace family had moved from Scotland in the 1500s, at a time when Northern Ireland was being targeted by King James I of England. He was keen to anglicise the Irish, and bring them into line. He offered incentives to the Irish chiefs to sell their land and gain his favour, and many were eager to make a profit and enjoy the rewards and protection offered by the King.

Scottish and English families seized the opportunity to buy the lands, believing in part that they were saving the Irish from themselves. In truth, this mass immigration was to bring about a change that would haunt the Irish for centuries. The Scots brought the Protestant message of John Knox and a language common with the English settlers, a change the King was intent on encouraging.

The journey was difficult for the Scottish families, uprooted from homes they had owned and occupied for many generations. The few possessions they were able to bring were packed in trunks then loaded onto long boats that offered little or no protection from the wind and weather as they sailed across the Irish Sea. At journey's end, the trunks were unloaded and put into handcarts available at the dock to be pulled to the 'promised land' grants.

The years proved this to have been a prosperous move for the Wallace family. Villages grew up around their plots and any animosity between the locals and the newcomers soon diffused. As long as men have sufficient food and shelter they prefer to befriend their neighbours and live in peace. Now times were hard and survival the main focus of thought and activity.

Before his death, Will Wallace had encouraged his two oldest sons, Arthur and John, to join the army. Wise council, because the boys sent money home to assist the family. After his father's untimely death James joined his older brothers to serve the Queen so the allotments paid from their soldier's pay packet could be increased. This allowance was of great assistance to Catherine.

"This is a quiet time for the army," James told her now, as they clustered around the kitchen table. "We have been called to guard convicts on the ship *Mayda* bound for Norfolk Island"

The family found it difficult to imagine the distance that would separate them, a journey twelve thousand miles across volatile oceans. Catherine couldn't help worrying about how she would keep herself and the youngest three children alive and feed throughout the coming winter, now her soldier sons were heading for the other side of the world.

Things were not improving in Ireland and none of them knew where the army would send its soldier-guards after the voyage to Norfolk Island. However,

Catherine would not allow them to dwell on how bad things were, encouraging them instead to pull together and enjoy each other's company. The brothers spent the days in long-overdue maintenance on the buildings, plastering walls and inserting new straw bundles into the roof to mend the thatch.

The evenings spent together brought much fun and laughter as they played charades with the youngsters. The soldiers acted out stories about their travels, winding tea towels around their heads and using strange accents as extra clues.

The children portrayed what their world had shrunk to: working long hours to grow potatoes that spoiled in the ground; fighting off those who were hungry and would steal from them if they could, or doing their lessons, so they could read and write to improve their chances in the future.

When the game changed to knucklebones, a favourite with the children, Catherine and Esther excused themselves to make tea and talk of women's matters. Esther was heavy with child and fearful about giving birth on the ship.

Catherine reached out and rested her hand on Esther's rounded belly as though she was talking to both mother and baby.

"John will look after you, and there'll be a ship's surgeon aboard. Be sure you walk on deck as often as the weather allows. Exercise, fresh air and sunshine are what makes for strong mothers and healthy babies. Don't forget women give birth aboard ships all over the world these days."

"That's what John tells me," Esther exclaimed. "But it's not him giving birth, it's me!" She clasped her mother-in-law's hand. "I know you're right and that John has made a good decision to pursue his career. Even though we don't know where the army will take us, it couldn't be worse than staying in Ireland when things are becoming so difficult."

"You're a wise and brave young woman, Esther. I hope one day I will meet my grandchild."

Catherine had warmly approved of her son's choice when he married Esther, a pretty girl and skilled at weaving and stitching clothes and hats. But her greatest asset was her common sense. She would support John and care for her family no matter where the couple ended up. The two women grew silent now, both knowing they had little control over the future and from now on must rely on faith and good luck.

Catherine knew that many folk in Ireland would end up in the workhouses being set up as relief for those who, in these hard times, could not feed themselves. The buildings were organised in a similar cruel and heartless fashion to those in England, where family members were separated the minute they entered.

Men, women and children were assigned to different living quarters. Some inmates were never to see their sons and daughters again. The poor suffered not only hunger and degradation, but also the loss of love and comfort that only comes from the family.

Staff were frequently ex-police or ex-army, callous attendants who saw no harm in pilfering food and cloth meant for the impoverished. The food served twice a day offered little nourishment. Porridge with milk or 'stirabout' – when potatoes were added - in the morning and, in the evening, watery soup. Children were given a third meal of bread.

Men were put to work breaking up rocks to repair old roads or make new ones. The women watched out of the windows as their men trudged off, shoulders drooped and heads bowed in shame. The women, too, had their allotted tasks – long hours of cleaning, cooking and sewing, mending clothes and making sacks.

Both women and children were assigned another duty they all detested: picking oakum. This entailed the tedious separating of strands of old rope for reuse, a job that would not jeopardise any commercial interests outside the workhouses because no one wanted such work. Fingers bled when the skin shredded from tugging at the threads of coarse rope.

Catherine hoped her family would not be among those driven to such desperation – her children forgetting any other life, their personality stifled by an institution that gave then no proper care or intellectual stimulation.

Arthur, John and James had good reason to worry about leaving their mother and siblings behind. Things would not improve in the years to follow, worsening for everyone in Ireland. Catherine's plot of land was small and only suitable for growing potatoes.

Owners of bigger farms grew grain, but the crops were not kept in Ireland to feed the nation's starving. Instead, it was exported to Europe where the grain crops had failed and a good profit could be made. One million people died in the coming years.

A million others were lucky enough to emigrate to England, there to find work as railroad navvies; or to America, the land of the free, thus saving themselves from starvation. Catherine and the children were not among the latter.

Chapter 9

The three Wallace brothers boarded the convict ship *Mayda* in London, in August 1845. They were to guard those referred to as 'the Milbank convicts.' Milbank Prison, built on the banks of the River Thames, was used to detain men before transportation to Norfolk Island.

The brothers might not have been called to guard duty in any other year, but by now the convict population on Norfolk Island had escalated to its highest number of nearly two thousand men.

The one hundred and ninety-nine prisoners they would be guarding on the *Mayda* were one-quarter of the total number transported in 1845.

The guards had much in common with the convicts they were in charge of. Both were leaving families behind, not knowing when or if they would see them again; and a journey on the ocean was almost as perilous for the guards as it was for the prisoners.

Some of the convicts had families on the dock, aching for a chance to catch a last glimpse of sons, brothers, sweethearts and husbands. There was even a last-minute bid to rescue one man from being sent to the colony. All pleas for mercy went unheeded and the ship set sail as ordered.

The guards stood on the deck overseeing the prisoners as the land dwindled into distance and disappeared along with the crowd that had gathered. One prisoner, an insignificant little fellow, began to play his mouth organ. William moved forward to discipline him, but the plaintive sounds of the *Londonderry Air* stirred the hearts of all, and he stepped back.

He recognised the deep and silent welling of grief among these reluctant passengers.

Esther delivered her baby during the third week of the journey. She demonstrated great courage, as so many women had to in such times. Childbirth was fraught with enough dangers without being asked to deliver in a claustrophobic cabin that never stopped rolling even when the sea was calm.

She had followed her mother-in-law's advice, taking walks in the fresh air whenever she could, a habit she enjoyed because it took her from the dreary cabin that offered little stimulus or comfort.

The surgeon, Dr Kilroy, was a competent man, and

her son Alex obliged by preferring the adventure of life to tarrying in the womb. He arrived on time and with little fuss on the 9th of September.

John looked down at his son, whose little face crumpled as though he was about to cry. The new father stroked the soft cheek with the back of his fingers.

"You're a bonny wee lad and I'm proud of your mam today."

The baby quietened as though he recognised the voice and approved of the compliment.

Esther rested her head on her husband's shoulder.

"There'll be no forgetting this day for either of us. It's quite a story to tell our son when he is grown. I look forward to getting a message to Catherine. She will be proud of her first grandson."

"Yes," said John thoughtfully, I'll see what I can do about sending a message from Norfolk Island."

"I'm looking forward to getting out of here for a walk on the deck. Do you think it'll be safe to take Alex out in a few days to get the air?"

"We'll see what the surgeon says. The prisoners are in a routine and discipline is good on board. So when you're stronger I'm sure it will be all right."

☆

John had noticed a close-knit group of prisoners, two older men and three younger, who seemed well-behaved - a good influence on the others, in fact. He decided to ask Kilroy about them.

"Four from one family," Kilroy explained. "They've given us no problems. All first-time offenders for burglary; married men with small children. The fifth man is a kindly fellow convicted for embezzlement. It was his supporters who caused the fuss on the dock before we sailed."

"That seems a bit tough," remarked John. "It's bad enough my brothers and I leaving our mother and siblings, but at least we're getting army pay and have a future to look forward to. There, but for the grace of God and a bit of Irish luck go any of us, if you ask me."

The Wallace family had their share of diarrhoea caused by the putrid water before they reached the Cape, but it was the prisoners who suffered most. They were undernourished and weakened before the trip began, unlike the soldiers who were always well-fed.

Esther kept baby Alex to a routine. She had plenty of rich milk and was able to feed him at regular times. She walked around the deck with him in her arms. He slept in the fresh air, and seemed to grow daily before her eyes.

Another woman went into labour two months after

Alex was born. She had suffered from the effects of the bad water and was already weakened. Even though she had fresh food and water now, and the help of the surgeon, the baby did not survive.

The mother laboured for many hours in vain, the cries tearing at Esther's heart. She could not imagine the pain of carrying a baby full term to lose him to an ocean burial.

Esther was almost relieved when she heard the mother had passed away a day later and was to be consigned to the ocean with her child.

The grief was soon put aside, however, when everyone's life was at risk from a storm that hit the ship. Esther was left on her own in the tiny cabin while the men struggled to keep the ship afloat. The bunk and side cabinet were attached to the deck so Esther held young Alex to her breast with one hand and gripped the side of the bunk with the other.

Their travel trunk slid from one side of the cabin to the other, crashing and tipping, then settling back to be still before sliding again. Esther, still emotional after the birth, found herself struggling to remain calm.

Her imagination ran wild worrying for her family and the prisoners on the bottom deck. She imagined them clinging to their bunks, some vomiting, others cursing. She worried for those on deck and those manning the pumps below.

Would the storm never end?

Would this long night be her last?

Eventually all was calm, and the *Mayda* finally arrived at its destination on 8th January 1846, and put to anchor off Norfolk Island. The captain saw the prisoners safely ashore on the whaling boats and stayed for a few days to deal with the paperwork.

When the captain returned to the *Mayda* he had new orders for the soldiers. They were to travel to Sydney and meet up with their 65th Regiment, or Royal Bengal Tigers as they were known. There were no wars of any note for Britain at this time, so the regiment was to go to New Zealand to settle some skirmishes with the natives.

"It could take a while to calm these Maori down," mused Arthur, by now well-accustomed to army life. "From what I have heard, they're a determined lot and know how to put up a good fight."

"Yes," said James, "this might be where I take leave of Her Majesty's generosity."

He was young and had only joined for the pay and to escape the deprived conditions in Ireland.

John remained quiet for a while, pondering the two different reactions his brothers had to the new orders.

"Best we see how things go in New Zealand, but I've heard it's a land of opportunity, and with a young 'un to look after I may be joining you, James."

"Plenty of time to decide," said Arthur. "We will have some time to fill in Sydney, while we wait for the *Java* to pick us up. Best we make the most of our freedom, I'm thinking."

Arthur took his own advice seriously, because while they were in Sydney he met Mary Plunket, who had come from Dublin as a dairy maid. Mary was looking to take a step up in the world. She did not enjoy working in Australia with the heat and the flies; there were no good memories for her here.

It was not unusual for under-privileged women to seek out soldiers to marry. The military provided a regular wage and a secure life style. Mary was hoping to put the misery and degradation of poverty behind her.

Men outnumbered women about four to one in the colonies, which put women at risk of being improperly propositioned. The same statistics made it difficult for men like Arthur to find a suitable bride. Arthur found peace in Mary's company and relief from the worries of his family left behind in Ireland She was an attractive woman with a sharp tongue, a sharper mind and strength of character to match.

A soldier needed a wife who was strong-willed and able to cope on her own for long periods when he was away from home. There was one thing that concerned him. The Wallace family had stayed strong in the faith they had taken to Ireland so many years ago.

The Presbyterian Church had remained an important part of their lives. Mary was Catholic so the union would not have been tolerated in Ireland.

These were not normal times and Arthur didn't think the restrictions of the church would follow them this many miles from the priests in Ireland. Arthur had made his decision.

This woman would be the mother of his children and he believed the two of them would make a success of their lives together in New Zealand.

With his brothers, sister in law, and tiny nephew by his side he married Mary. So it was that Catherine's boys, Arthur, aged twenty-eight, with his new wife Mary; John, twenty-six, with his wife Esther, and son Alex; and James, only nineteen years old, sailed on the military ship, *Java*, to Korokorere in the Bay of Islands, New Zealand.

The ship didn't stay long in Korokorere, but time enough for the soldiers to wonder what this new country would be like. The town of Korokorere lies on a narrow peninsula where the pohutukawa trees spread their branches along the shoreline; a blaze of red flowers against dark green leaves heralding the summer, early flowers indicating a long dry season.

The town boasted a view no matter where you

looked, across the sea to the mainland or towards little islands dotted in all directions. The inhabitants were a mixture of whalers, soldiers, Maori and missionaries, with men outnumbering the women.

The wives of merchants and politicians were fine ladies, who brought along governesses to teach their children.

Settlers frequented the grog shops along the shore, bars full of drunk and foul-mouthed sailors along with women who came to make their fortune by satisfying the longings of men far from their homes.

The Wallace family was pleased when the ship sailed on towards the army barracks in Porirua, near Wellington. They were keen to settle down and get this war over as soon as possible.

Chapter 10

Mary settled well into army life and was thrilled when Arthur arranged for them to live in a house in Manners Street, Wellington.

There was not much flat land in Wellington, but this house was right on the beach. Hills rose steeply from the flats and were covered in dark and dense bush, which was being cleared as the need arose. Houses were compact and built not completely of timber, but with a wooden frame covered in raupo.

The cooking was done outside in a covered area in three-legged iron pots over a fire. Mary purchased fish and vegetables from Maori at first, but it wasn't long before she had a garden growing with vegetables and flowers, a reminder of home.

Life became easier with time and the couple's love grew and so did the family. The first born was William, named after Arthur's father, then Richard, followed by John, called Jack.

The town named after the Duke of Wellington had become quieter and safer since the earlier settlements of 1840.

Arthur and Mary were told the stories of how the valuable land was bought by the New Zealand Company with the intention of making this town the capital of New Zealand. But even before the cooking pots, soap, axes, fish hooks, clothing, pencils and the more valuable guns and ammunition were paid to Maori, pakeha surveyors were trampling through native homes and burial grounds, hammering in survey pegs.

Mary understood how Maori families felt, and did not hold back from speaking her mind on the matter.

"No wonder there has been trouble. Who can blame them for standing their ground and protecting what belongs to them?"

John and James didn't take long to see the sense in buying themselves out of the army. When they landed in Porirua they were given little time to dump their luggage in tents before the call to fall in at two o'clock. in the morning. From here they were sent straight into the bush to engage the enemy in unfamiliar terrain.

The fighting was at close quarters against warriors with fearsome faces covered in tattoos. The battle continued for two months, then the detachments were transferred to Whanganui.

Here the brothers gladly paid over their twenty pounds and began a civilian life in the developing township.

☆

Arthur and Mary watched the country grow and change over the next ten years. The bush was cleared and a better house built for Mary with an inside kitchen and bedrooms for the boys. Arthur would sit with his boys and tell them how he grew up on a farm in a land far away. He talked of planting potatoes in the fields, and how he milked the old house cow and fed the chickens.

He spoke with reverence of his mother and told his boys what a strong and intelligent woman she had to be to keep her family safe during difficult times. He told how his father had encouraged him to become a soldier, and what a brave man their grandfather was, giving his life to defend his family and property.

Arthur never spoke to anyone about the fear he felt for his mother and the siblings he said goodbye to for the last time, so long ago, but Mary understood his heart was heavy because he would never know their fate.

There were plenty of highlights in the growing city to keep Mary amused. Garden parties at Lady Grey's house and events along the beach front near the family's home.

The boys had a completely different life to their father and mother. Wellington had the sea before it and the bush behind, and plenty of places for young boys to hunt and play. They made friends with boys from many countries, settlers from Scotland, Ireland, England and other European countries, as well as the local Maori boys.

All the children picked up different customs and sayings from each other and they learned words in Maori te reo. The better they could communicate, the more fun they had, learning how to catch fish or find their way in the bush. The boys often visited Johnny Martin's store to buy sweets and every Sunday they attended St Peter's Sunday school for bible lessons.

A favourite outing was to the races along the beach near Lyall Bay and Island Bay. The settlers turned up in bullock drays and wagons for this spectacular annual event. Fine horses and even donkeys raced and there were toffee apples and fruit drinks on sale.

Maori children invited the Wallace boys to their whare, where the family slept on flax mats woven with delicate patterns. They learned to play stick games where each player held two sticks which were tapped on the ground then together then passed to the player opposite them without dropping the sticks. This required skill and was done while singing songs, slowly at first but getting faster until someone made a mistake and dropped a stick. The boys did not always tell their parents where they had been because they were not supposed to get too friendly with Maori.

"You must understand, I am paid to fight against the Maori, and it's best to keep your distance."

"But you don't fight the Maori in the towns," the boys protested, "and you don't fight kids."

"That is true, but things can change quickly in a new country."

The boys shrugged and tried to keep out of their parent's sight.

Arthur was kept occupied settling skirmishes with Maori. The 65th Regiment was to see more service than any other regiment in the New Zealand Land Wars. He wore the badge of the striped tiger with pride. There was mutual respect between the regiment and the Maori warriors, and there were times when the battle was motivated by duty rather than a will to conquer.

The 65th or '*hiketi pips*,' as Maori referred to them, was made up of more Irish than English soldiers. So along with the warrior pride of Maori, there was a certain relish in the tactical battles that prevailed.

Mary was happy and managed to fashion a good life for herself. She worshipped with Father O'Reilly at the Roman Catholic Chapel, St Mary of the Angels, further along Manners Street. But the children were baptised in St Peter's with the Reverend Cole, who along with Father O'Reilly showed remarkable tolerance and understanding for mixed marriages.

They knew that this was bound to occur because in a small population there wasn't the luxury of choice, making it difficult for people to marry within the faith, something that happened more and more often.

The New Zealand Company became intent on developing Whanganui. Unfortunately, this brought the land battles to the fore once more, and it was no surprise to Arthur when the order came for him to move there and relieve a company of the 58th Regiment.

Mary was worried about moving to the underdeveloped town and making a new home and garden. She did not look forward to what the upheaval would mean for the children.

In a desperate effort to delay the move, she reminded Arthur of the Gilfillan massacre in Matarawa, near Whanganui, which had horrified the military community soon after Mary and Arthur arrived in New Zealand. Mary remembered the massacre vividly because some of the children were the same age as her own and Mrs Gilfillan was also named Mary.

In 1847 John and Mary Gilfillan's family of seven and a neighbour's boy were enjoying a fine Sunday in April. They had put clothes out on the lawn to bleach in the sun. When John Gilfillan saw a group of Maori coming down out of the bush, he went into the house and asked his wife to send the children to fetch the clothes inside.

He went out to greet the group, offering tobacco to those who wanted it. He introduced them to his young son also called John, who had followed him out of the house. There was no sign of trouble. Maori asked for firewood and food; they were given the firewood, but were told the family did not have enough food to share.

Without warning a native struck the back of John's head with a tomahawk. Mary Gilfillan opened the door and pulled her husband and son to safety. She bound the wound and pleaded with her husband to leave the house and go for help.

"We will be safe," she assured her husband. "Our family will come to no harm. The natives have never hurt women and children. You must leave; it is you they want to harm, not us."

As dusk fell John climbed out the window and set off to the neighbour's farm four miles away. Mary took the children to the bedroom and hid them under the beds where she believed they would be safe until the natives went on their way. But the Maori began to break the windows and rammed a stick through the clay wall of the bedroom.

This was out of character and for the first time Mary realised neither she nor the children were safe. She signalled to her daughter, another Mary, to bundle her baby Agnes in a blanket and climb out the window as quietly as she could and head for safety.

The mother watched as her daughter ran towards cover. She did not even flinch as a weapon was raised, hitting her daughter, then aimed at the baby.

Mary waited a while, without showing any fear or concern that would alarm the younger children. She indicated that each of them should climb out of the window and run for their lives. By the time the last two children, Sara and young John, made their escape, it was dark.

The front end of the house had been set on fire, giving some light for the two to see where they were going.

Sara felt a wooden weapon hit her shoulder and she fell into a ditch on top of her brother, where they were left for dead. Sara carefully raised her head to find her mother. She saw her running across the grass in her light-coloured dress, then she heard a scream and Mary fell.

Maori stood over her with tomahawks held high.

Sara and John crept away from the ditch and soon found their sister Mary holding the baby, both drenched in blood. The baby died later in hospital, bringing the death toll to six, viciously murdered in the worst episode yet seen in New Zealand.

Arthur tried to quell Mary's fears. He reminded her that the massacre was a long time ago, and they had been lucky to live in one place for so long.

"We will be joining John and Esther, and James, in Whanganui. It's a town that's going ahead. Shops are being built – Taylor and Watts sells everything from a needle to an anchor – and new settlers are arriving every day."

Whanganui was built on the river of the same name, a river that has its source in Mount Tongariro. First the police station was built, then the magistrate's house, followed by small thatched houses, spreading along the water's edge.

To Mary, the town seemed primitive and more threatening than Wellington where she had a circle of friends. She watched with concern as the new settlers, who had sailed to Wellington, arrived on foot after the long and difficult walk around the coast.

Did the new immigrants have any idea what they were coming to?

The Maori around the mouth of the river and the town were generally friendly and happy to trade potatoes and pigs for tobacco. But Maori from up-river were hostile and wanted to protect the land that was being surveyed for the white man. Mary knew there was good reason she should be fearful for her children.

About a year after the move to Whanganui, Arthur realised his battles were not only on the battle field against the Maori, but on the home front as well. Whanganui had a zealous Catholic priest named Father Jean Pezant, who had first settled in Akaroa ministering to the French settlers and converting the South Island Maori. Pezant had become a good friend of Bishop Pompallier, the well-known French missionary from the Bay of Islands.

Pompallier and Pezant had worked together encouraging French rule in Akaroa during a standoff between the French and British. The Church had hopes of seeing the French take what they considered rightful governance of the South Island because this would allow easy access to convert the natives.

The two priests later travelled together, Pezant becoming a student of Pompallier. Pezant was an industrious man and built many churches around New Zealand, including the well-known Sacred Heart of St

Mary in Whanganui. He engaged the 18th and 65th Regiments to help with the building in Whanganui; an interesting choice, given what followed.

He was a man who expressed his views forcibly; among them his distaste for the 'sin' of mixed marriage. He went as far as telling Mary, her marriage was null and void.

Arthur consoled Mary, reminding her of her situation back in Sydney.

"It was not easy for you to make an honest life for yourself, don't forget that. You and I have built a good home for our boys in a land that offers more than the confines of religion. Don't be fooled by a priest who knows nothing of what we have been through, yet interferes in matters between husband and wife."

Mary lifted her chin with the determination Arthur had learned to admire.

"You are right. We have lived as man and wife for ten years and I am proud our boys have your name. This is a new land and new rules apply. We can live as we desire. Our children are wrapped in God's love, no matter where we worship."

Arthur put his arms around Mary.

"You are right. Let's put an end to this foolishness for good. Remember, we made a sacred promise to each other, blessed by God. We have loved each other and lain together to make babies."

Arthur lifted Mary into his arms and carried her to their bed. There they held each other close, and talked about the children and how happy they had been. They made love as if for the first time.

Afterwards they continued to caress each other's body as they spoke of their plans and dreams. They both renewed the commitment they had made with one another and believed their love would sustain their marriage above all interference.

Arthur drew Mary to him again and kissed her with a passion she had not felt before. Her body responded as the fire of love burned within her, and she knew instinctively she would be with child. Mary hoped this would be a girl to complete the family.

But the priest was a determined and persistent man and once the pregnancy became obvious, he would not be happy until the baby was baptised into the Catholic faith. Mary tried to stay true to Arthur, but the priest convinced her that she should not use Arthur's name for the new baby. This would be proof, he told her, that she was a 'good Catholic.' Baby Elizabeth was born and baptised in the Sacred Heart of St Mary, with the parents recorded as Arthur Wallace and Mary Plunket, Mary returning to her maiden name.

Arthur confronted the priest.

"The Bible teaches that no man should come

between husband and wife, and yet you have used religion to cause shame and confusion for my wife and the mother of my children."

The priest was taken aback by the attack but his work was done. He knew that this child Elizabeth would hold to the faith and raise her children as Catholic. Two years later Mary had another son, Archie, baptised as a Protestant like his brothers. Sadly, the threads holding the marriage together were eroding, and the rift between them grew.

The trouble over Maori land was also escalating and the fighting took Arthur away from his family for longer periods of time.

Mary went where she felt she had support, spending more time on church activities. This led her to befriend a man from Arthur's regiment who had helped with the building of The Sacred Heart of St Mary. It was not long before the friendship was seen by the priest as a means for Mary to correct her wrong-doing and become legitimately married.

Her marriage to Arthur was annulled, and all the children moved with Mary to her catholic husband's farm along the Whanganui River. The priest had won now all the children were under his influence.

Arthur was left with nothing but the ongoing wars to take his mind off the wrong that had been done and the sadness that filled his life. Arthur's older boys were aware of the injustice, and soon after his mother remarried, William left home. He was only twelve years old, but found work on a dairy farm at Kai Iwi where he lived in a clay house thatched with straw interlaced with nikau fronds, a warm and sturdy residence.

Four years later he joined the Kai Iwi Volunteer Cavalry to fight against Maori like his father.

After his divorce, Arthur's escapades led him north through New Plymouth, where he fought against Wiremu Kingi at Waitara.

Kingi was not interested in war, but was opposed to the government buying the 600 acre Pekapeka block at the mouth of the Waitara River.

Arthur was hospitalised several times in battle, but went on to fight in the Ngaruawahia, Tuakau and Orakau engagements before his discharge in 1864 because of chronic rheumatism.

Arthur, though, had not finished with army life. Despite his obvious discomfort, he enlisted in the Colonial Army Whanganui Regiment of Militia and was posted to Marton in the Rangitikei district. He served twenty-three years, seventeen and a half of them in New Zealand.

He was awarded two medals, the New Zealand Cross and the Royal New Zealand Army Veteran's Cross. Later he was offered work with Major Marshall, who owned Tutu Totara Station, just out of Marton.

He was happy there, enjoying the garden parties and social life on the station that he was part of until his death in August 1876, thirty-one years after leaving his family in Ireland.

Arthur's brother John had worked hard in civilian life. He had been granted land on No 2 line. Esther had three more sons after Alex and four daughters.

In 1885 they bought the Gilfillan farm, opposite their property, and made a courageous decision to build a clay house near the home that had been destroyed during the massacre.

Brother James moved away from Whanganui to New Plymouth where Arthur had spent many years fighting over land settlements, battles that James was pleased not to be engaged in.

Chapter 11

Arthur's oldest son William became a respected soldier like his father. He fought in many West Coast engagements but the turning point in what was to become an illustrious career was when he rode as a youth in the cavalry charge in Opotiki.

This was one of very few cavalry charges in the New Zealand Land Wars. When the selection was being made William, still young and of slim build, was overlooked by his commanding officer.

His sergeant spoke up for him.

"What about Wallace, sir? He's a capital horseman."

Wallace went on to fight beside men who were, in his own words, 'a splendid crowd of cavalry men.' Often they were the younger and well-educated sons of wealthy families.

He served under Baron von Tempsky, a Prussian soldier who had trained to be a Forest Ranger with

Captain Jackson. The Forest Rangers were set up in August 1863 to fight Maori in the bush where battles were fought at close range.

The Rangers carried special weapons, the shorter carbine rifle, revolvers and a specially made hand weapon similar to the Bowie knife. The knife was used for chopping a path in the forest, cutting firewood or warding off an attacker's blow while the revolver was used in the other hand. All the weapons were perfect for guerrilla-tactics against Maori in their own territory.

There were only a hundred men in the Rangers at any time because of a shortage of the special weapons. By November 1863 the Forest Rangers were disbanded, but it soon became obvious that the army could not do without them. Their success in warding off Maori who were attacking the ships carrying food to the troops along the Waikato River was crucial.

Jackson was authorised to form a new company, to carry on the defence. A few days later Von – as he was known by his men – was promoted to Captain and asked to form a second company.

Von Tempsky's nature was the complete opposite of his superior. Captain Jackson had trained his team in the manner of a true military man, cautious and concerned for the safety of his troops. Von Tempsky was a soldier of fortune, who had been involved in pursuits that included gold mining in California, Bendigo and, more recently, the Coromandel Peninsula where he was also employed as a newspaper correspondent.

A flashy dresser, he was more interested in self-promotion, admiration and glory, but no one could deny his enthusiasm. Known to Maori as Manurau, 'the bird that flits everywhere,' his skills lay in building a loyal team, and inspiring his men rather than in adhering to the true military model.

By 1865 Jackson had resigned and von Tempsky, now a major, was in full command of the Forest Rangers, who were about to become involved in the Second Taranaki War. At around this time the commanders of the British troops began to view such wars as unnecessary engagements for a self-serving New Zealand Government, so in mid-1866 the Forest Rangers were disbanded for good.

A disappointed von Tempsky was asked to take charge of No. 5 Division of the armed constabulary, which included men from the Whanganui Yeomanry Cavalry where William Wallace and his younger brother Richard were serving.

Soon after this appointment, Wallace was ordered to escort a cart from Round Bush near Hawera through Hauhau territory to Waihi. The cart was loaded with fresh meat and bread, as well as a badly injured soldier named Mick.

The Hauhau were a tribe under the leadership of the prophet Te Ua Haumene, who mixed teachings from the Old Testament with traditional Maori beliefs and observances. The Hauhau were strongly opposed to the land being taken from them as more settlers moved into the area.

Private Tuffin was driving, and Wallace rode ahead with Private Haggerty, and Private Noonan followed as rear guard. The road was rough and the going slow because Mick, the wounded man, was in a bad way.

Wallace was aware of the risk of attack.

"Keep your eyes peeled," he ordered "The Hauhau will be keen to stop our supplies getting through."

The bush was thick and the Hauhau warriors waited in silence, not attacking until the soldiers were nearly upon them. Twenty Maori ambushed the convoy. Haggerty's horse was the first victim, though it took several bullets to bring it down. Haggerty was thrown to the ground. He tried to run, but had been wounded by a bullet in the leg. The warriors sprang from cover and were onto him in seconds. Haggerty stood no chance as tomahawks took their gruesome toll.

Wallace was next for the slaughter. Natives ran towards him with tomahawks held high. He fired his pistol, then the carbine, wounding one, killing another and slowing the rest of them down.

Then by some miracle the warriors turned their attention to the cart horses. They shot the shaft horse, cut the lead horse free, and one of the injured Hauhau rode it away. The driver Tuffin was unarmed and made a run for it, heading to the Waihi Redoubt.

The wounded soldier stumbled out of the horseless cart, but his injuries were so debilitating he was unable to mount a horse. Summing up the situation, he realised immediately the predicament he was in. He begged the remaining soldiers for protection from the Hauhaus' tomahawks.

"It's okay, Mick," Wallace shouted. "We won't leave you. Get between my horse and Noonan's and we'll keep you covered until a rescue party finds us."

By 1868 Chief Titokowaru was causing plenty of trouble in the Hawera area. This was a battle von Tempsky was looking forward to; a worthy foe indeed. The chief spoke perfect English thanks to his missionary education and had studied military battles in the history books. Titokowaru was more than a match for his opponents.

William and Richard Wallace knew there would be many casualties on both sides. The site was Te Ngutu o te manu (The Bird's Beak). The village had been burned in the 1866 expedition and had not been rebuilt. Instead, a large settlement had been set up in a clearing across the river. William was to retell the story many times.

"It was raining and the stream was high, but we crossed and mounted the bank on the other side where we faced palisading of tall timber. It was a half-moon shape with the convex side towards us.

"The Hauhau fired a volley, wounding two men. I ordered my brother Richard to the rear rank, and moved the men towards the stockade. There were small openings, just big enough for a man to crawl through. I poked my head into the hole fully aware that I was a perfect target. I surveyed the area. The ground was overgrown, providing negligible protection, but there were a few rata and mohe trees dotted about.

"The whare had been built in the middle of the clearing so the lack of good cover was of concern. We moved forward keeping low and covering each other as we crossed the clearing. We were under heavy fire as the warriors tried to keep us at bay, then word came through that one of our men was down.

"A soldier ran up from the rear and yelled. 'It's the bugler, Private Wallace. He's hit bad.'

"I ran back and bent over my brother; he had been hit in the jugular. Blood spurted from the wound that would bring his death. I held his head in my arms, and looked into his eyes. He recognised me. I could feel a wave of relief spread through his body; he would not die alone. There was nothing the medics could do. Too soon he sunk into his final sleep. I lay his head on the damp grass and returned to my men.

"The fighting was intense and bloody, but we made our way forward to the large meeting house and set it on fire. I was about to retire my men when one brave soldier volunteered to use the last of the hand grenades we had brought. The rest of us retreated to where Richard had fallen. I looked towards the battle ground and watched as the soldier threw grenades into the small openings of the whare. I became acutely aware of the futility of battle. Brothers were being killed on both sides, and for what? I picked my brother up and carried him out to be buried from a church, the way his mother would want."

William's brother Richard had joined the volunteers as soon as he was old enough. He was seventeen years of age when he fell in the battle of Te Ngutu o te manu.

Richard was to become folklore through a poem written about the battle by an officer, Lieutenant Hastings, this verse describing his last moments of life:

Another Wallace 'twas his fate, he nobly fought
  and nobly fell.
The bugle's voice and the Maori yell

The government was eager to put an end the conflict in the Taranaki area and was putting pressure on the soldiers to make a premature attack on Titokowaru's main pa.

The day following Richard's death, von Tempsky and McDonnell made strategic plans that they believed would defeat the Chief. Titokowaru was prepared and the militia came under heavy and accurate fire from warriors in a maze of trenches seeming to appear from nowhere. Some were hidden in hollowed out trees, causing many casualties.

Titokowaru waited patiently as the soldiers advanced then shouted this order, several times, "surround the soldiers!"

McDonnell knew the best course of action was to retire while there was still a chance of carrying the wounded to safety. He gave the order to retreat and headed towards von Tempsky, who was outside the warrior's encirclement and unaware of the number of casualties the militia had sustained. Von Tempsky wasn't interested in backing down. Here was an opportunity to win this battle and the Victoria Cross he had long coveted. He advanced, but the Maori who had followed McDonnell were now within half a chain of where he stood.

A warrior fired and shot one of von Tempsky's men. Von Tempsky went to the aid of his soldier and within seconds was shot dead with a bullet through the forehead. His life was lost to his search for glory, which went instead to the three Maori warriors who had fired upon him.

The natives did not know which of them had fired the fatal bullet, but all would be held in the highest regard for toppling a leader with the mana of this flamboyant soldier.

New Zealand lost a versatile and courageous soldier who had earned unwavering loyalty from his men, a talented artist and writer, who would have written well of his opponent Titokowaru and the highly-trained warriors who took his life.

William lost a brother and his commander to the battles at Te Ngutu o te manu. He had learned the pain of death in a sad chapter in his army career. He had developed great respect for Maori for their tactical skills over the years. For this reason, he did not give any encouragement to his younger brother when Jack decided to leave his mother's home and join the Kai Iwi Volunteer Cavalry to fight the Maori like his brothers.

Jack was proud to join the cavalry, regarding his brothers as true men of courage. The admiration he held for his father and his two brothers was stronger than the warnings of his family. His cavalry training included the trade of blacksmithing, which stood him in good stead after the tiresome wars ended one year later.

Jack's sister, Elizabeth Plunket, met and married John Maitland Brough. John and Elizabeth had purchased land in Banks Peninsula in the South Island and suggested Elizabeth's two brothers join them.

Jack was at a loose end so the brothers followed their sister and started a blacksmith and wheelwright business in Duvauchelle, Banks Peninsula.

William, after a period of mourning, married his brother Richard's girlfriend, Mary Jane Wallace, the daughter of his Uncle John and Aunt Esther. Together they raised a family on land awarded to him in the Whanganui area.

The family finally settled in Meremere where they bought a farm surrounded by native bush that William ensured was preserved.

Part 2:
Akaroa

Chapter 12

Kandel in Germany, 1840

Johann and Eva Breitmeyer travelled one thousand miles from Kandel in Germany, crossing France to reach the busy port of Rochefort. Johann was determined to escape hard times and an unstable government in his homeland. Eva was reluctant to leave her home at first, but deep down she agreed with her husband.

Their four children, Johann, Katerina, Elizabeth and George, would be better off if they took this opportunity to emigrate to Akaroa on the Banks Peninsula, in the South Island of New Zealand. They had heard from a traveller visiting the village about a company that would ship them for free.

Christian Jakob Wackearle, a journeyman-locksmith from Baden, was determined to spread the news about his impending journey to New Zealand.

"Free transport as well as five acres of productive

land for every male, and two and a half acres for every boy between ten and fifteen years old," he exclaimed, as though he still didn't quite believe it himself.

"The company supplies rations of food for every person over a period of eighteen months on the proviso the land is cleared and productive within that time. And you are entitled to half of any extra land cleared during the five years. I'm booked. This is too good to miss."

Without doubt it was an excellent opportunity, made possible by a French whaler, Captain Langlois, who had seen the potential in the South Island of New Zealand while he was whaling in the Pacific. He was particularly drawn to Kāi Tahu (Akaroa Harbour) on Banks Peninsula where he and others anchored whaling vessels.

The harbour was as beautiful as any he had seen. Lush green bush grew on the hillsides, spilling down almost to the water's edge. The clear notes of tui and pigeons filled the air with melodic song.

Langlois had found the local Maori amicable, intelligent and good trading partners. Some joined the French and American whaling ships and became multilingual. In 1838 Langlois made what was to turn out to be a risky investment. He purchased land from the local chiefs before travelling back to France to convince the government of his ambition to colonise the South Island for King Louis Philippe I.

He was aware of the need to proceed as quickly as possible because the British were well established in the far north settlement of Kororareka and intent on colonising the North Island. Langlois was afraid they might turn their minds towards the South Island.

The project needed financial backing that should have been easy to obtain considering the riches that were on offer from whaling in the southern Pacific Ocean. In the event, making a deal proved difficult, with one of the more substantial backers changing his mind after lengthy negotiations.

Langlois was out of his depth in dealing with these high-powered businessmen, and it was easy for remaining investors to blame him for the breakdown in the deal.

To his credit, Langlois did manage to broker an agreement with another group of several men, many of whom came from the cities of Nantes and Bordeaux. They formed a company that became known by two names, the French New Zealand Company, and the more commonly used Nanto-Bordelaise Company after the two French cities.

Pierre Joseph Sainte-Croix Crocquet de Belligny, an eminent scientist sponsored by the Natural History Museum of Paris, was chosen as the representative of the company in New Zealand. The company was impressed with Belligny and believed he was the best man to manage their financial interests. He was to be responsible for purchasing tools and equipment to be made available through the company store when they landed, at a cost, of course.

The company began to pay too much attention to Belligny, effectively squeezing the Captain out. Langlois was understandably angered by this shift in loyalty and a wedge was driven between the two men that would later become a rift. Langlois stood his ground, making it absolutely clear that it was his land purchase making colonisation a plausible venture.

By now King Louis Philippe I was convinced that if he didn't colonise the South Island he would end up losing profits in customs tax paid to the English. He was also considering new territory for a penal colony in the southern seas, though undecided about exactly where that should be sited. An agreement was at last signed that suited all parties: the King, the government, Langlois and the newly-formed company.

The King provided the naval ship *Mahé* to be loaned to Captain Langlois to transport the emigrants. The *Mahé* was sent to Rochefort, an old port on the Charente River. The dock had once been the largest naval port in the world so a city had grown up around the port, neat and tidy, with its streets facing the shore.

The *Mahé* was refitted to make her suitable for passengers and allow space to carry the many supplies and animals they would need to survive in the new land. The ship was renamed the *Comte de Paris* and was to be used later by Langlois to continue his whaling expeditions.

Finding colonists was interesting because recruiting had to be done secretly to keep their plans from the British government. The British had recently named William Hobson to be their diplomatic representative for New Zealand and it had been hinted that he had his eye on at least the top half of the South Island. So, apart from a small advertisement placed in the local paper in Rochefort – without official permission – the opportunity to travel to the other side of the world was spread by word of mouth.

Times were difficult for the French peasants who were poor and hungry. Failing wheat crops had reduced them to a meagre diet, consisting mainly of gruel. Among these desperate folk, there were some who were brave and adventurous, willing to pit their talents against all odds to improve their lives. Folk like these, who had seen the advertisement or heard whispers of the deal from friends, filled the berths on the *Comte de Paris.*

Most were from France, but word had spread across the border to Germany and one man found his way from Belgium. Their numbers made up of half married couples, half single men and one brave single woman. Each offered talents that would enhance the new settlement: seamstresses, carpenters, bakers, farmers, gardeners, sawyers; all willing to work hard together. Johann Breitmeyer was a shoemaker, and his friend and countryman was the travelling locksmith.

Pierre Belligny, acting as agent for the Nanto-Bordelaise Company, travelled with the passengers so that he could look after the provisions.

Captain Langlois was responsible for the care of the settlers and even though he was not on easy terms with Belligny, whom he blamed for his ever-increasing decline in popularity with the company, he arranged for the latter to continue with those duties once they landed any time he was absent.

The settlers were to be protected by a naval presence. The King arranged for the naval corvette the *Aube* captained by Charles François Lavaud to leave ahead of the *Comte de Paris*. Lavaud, the King's Commissioner, was given instructions to set up a naval base at Akaroa and hold the territory, until the settlers arrived. The ship was to remain and assist in setting up the colony.

Part of the plan to strengthen the bid for colonisation was to land missionaries as the British had done in the North Island.

For this reason, the *Aube* carried four Marist missionaries: Fathers Jean Pezant, Jean-André Tripe and Brothers Duperron and Bertrand who were to be dropped off at Hobart enroute to Akaroa to catch a ship bound for Kororareka in the North Island. There they would meet with the well-established Catholic missionary, Jean Baptiste Pompallier, and travel to the South Island at a later date.

The *Comte de Paris* did not begin her voyage well. Before the ship's departure a woman passenger jumped overboard fully clothed. She was unable to swim and attempts to rescue her failed because of the weight of her clothes. She had chosen to die in the Charente River rather than travel to the ends of the earth with her husband. The episode was regarded as a bad omen by superstitious seamen, and their fears were seemingly confirmed when the ship sprang a leak.

This was only the beginning. The pilot took the ship to where she was able to continue under the captain's orders, but his boat was late coming to pick him up. The pilot was strongly averse to being stuck on a ship travelling to the other side of the world with a group of peasants so he ran the ship onto a sand bar.

The decision was understandable, but proved disastrous. The ship was so heavily laden, cargo had to be discharged to allow it to float off the bar. This required a return to the dock while cargo was reloaded.

While the reloading took place, Belligny noticed that Langlois had not earthed the lightning conductor on the main mast and reminded the captain that they were carrying gunpowder. This brought further friction in the relationship between the two men and a foolhardy response from Langlois, who refused to earth the mast.

He might have meant to order the work done later, but at this time he was more intent on taking revenge on Belligny as later, Belligny discovered that some of his personal belongings had mysteriously not been reloaded.

These two men would not have crossed paths in normal times. In a changing world where new lands were being discovered, men now lived by unwritten laws that took no account of class distinction.

Two weeks later the *Comte de Paris* set sail for the second time, though not without incident. Progress was slow because of difficulty in steering. An assessment would have to wait until they reached the Canary Islands to pick up supplies. Investigations found no fault with the rudder and it was decided the steering problem was a design fault, causing days to be added onto an already long journey.

From the Cape of Good Hope, the ill-fated ship with her weary travellers turned east towards their destination. Their luck seemed to change with the birth of a baby boy to Joseph and Madeleine Libeau, who named the baby Armand, after one of the ship's officers.

The baby, a brother for Catherine and Joseph, was a symbol of hope for the new beginning so eagerly anticipated by the passengers.

Unfortunately, the excitement was soon forgotten when on the night of 11th to 12th July the *Comte de Paris* hit a storm south-west of Tasmania. Katerina Breitmeyer was to relate the story many times to her children and grandchildren over the coming years.

"I was five and a bit when our ship struck the storm. The thunder crashed and the lightning flashed, brightening up the night sky. Then came the lightning bolt that hit our top mast. The mast creaked and groaned then fell crashing through the rigging and swoosh, it disappeared into the sea! Even the seamen were terrified, but not me, I was brave."

"Or I was, until another bolt struck the forward mast. This time the mast became entangled in the main mast. Now I was afraid because the ship rolled onto its side and everyone thought it was going to turn right over. My father saw us all to the cabin and insisted we stay there as the ship pitched and rolled making everything slide across the floor, scraping and twisting with the movement of the ship."

"The captain was used to storms and began to yell his urgent commands. Soon seamen were scrambling over the deck, cutting away the sails and freeing the mast. Passengers – men, women, and the older children – worked the bilge pumps until the ship was level again. We were all relieved when the storm stopped and we could open the portholes. Well, all of us except my friend Joseph Libeau because he put his head out the porthole and his new cap blew away."

The storm damage delayed the ship further as she limped across the Tasman Sea with nothing but her mainsail and some makeshift work on the two missing masts.

On the day the *Comte de Paris* was battered by the storm, an even worse delay in making a bid to colonise the South Island for France was to occur. Lavaud sailed the *Aube* into Kororareka instead of Akaroa Bay as he ordered. He had made the fateful decision to bypass Hobart and drop the missionaries directly to their North Island destination where they were to meet with Pompallier.

Lavaud was surprised to find Captain Stanley of the British ship *Britomart* moored in the harbour. Lavaud would already be regretting his decision not to proceed straight to Akaroa. Meetings with Captain

Stanley were cordial and informative. The *Britomart*, he was told, would be sailing to Wellington on 22nd July, with two magistrates, Murphy and Robinson, to hold court in the city.

The *Aube* was a faster vessel than the *Britomart* and Lavaud left port a few days later confident he would reach Akaroa in time to prepare for the arrival of the *Comte de Paris* before any intervention from the British ship, which he believed was heading to Wellington.

As the *Aube* drew close to Akaroa, luck abandoned the captain. The weather turned nasty, making it impossible to enter the harbour mouth. He hung back waiting for the wind to change, not knowing that the crippled *Comte de Paris* had reached New Zealand, and was also caught outside the harbour, and was now anchored at Pigeon Bay.

Two male passengers who had died of scurvy were taken ashore for burial and fresh water was brought aboard. The journey had been long from its last port of call on the coast of West Africa.

When the *Aube* finally sailed into Akaroa harbour on 15th August, Lavaud discovered the *Britomart* had not sailed to Wellington but straight to Akaroa from Kororareka, arriving on 10th August. The next day the magistrates Murphy and Robinson had hoisted the British flag and held court.

The *Comte de Paris* was held up until 18th August because Langlois was confirming his agreement with Maori chiefs who had paddled out in their waka to meet with their old friend at Pigeon Bay!

Both the French ships had arrived too late.

Much had happened since the emigrants sailed from Rochefort. Captain Hobson had been busy working for his Queen. He had managed to coerce forty Maori chiefs to sign the Treaty of Waitangi on 6th February 1840, thus declaring the North Island a British colony.

Copies of the Treaty were carried to chiefs in other parts of New Zealand to sign over the following months. The two southern islands would be claimed by right of discovery by Captain Cook; an unconvincing argument that would be hotly debated in the near future.

Lavaud's visit to Kororareka did nothing to improve the situation when he let slip that the *Comte de Paris* followed close behind and was carrying settlers.

Chapter 13

The settlers were surprised and disturbed by the sight of a British ship and the British flag flying on the shoreline. Langlois still believed he could claim the land for the French. He assured the settlers that he would put things to right and encouraged them to go ashore despite the inclement weather, and the Union Jack fluttering in the wind.

Not one of the passengers had the stomach for the only alternative option, which was to remain on board and return to France, and all stepped ashore on 19th August 1840.

The crew of the *Aube* and the *Comte de Paris* erected three tents: one for the married couples and the single woman, one for the bachelors, and the third for storage. The weather was still bleak, with a temperature of 8° celsius, with continuous wind and rain an unwelcoming introduction to their new home.

Johann and Eva Breitmeyer found little comfort on

their first night ashore. The family's clothes were damp and the children were fractious. Few of the settlers slept that night. Anxious and disappointed they worried what the future held for them.

"Have we done the right thing?"

Eva's whispered words misted in the cold night air.

"We certainly won't make a judgment this night, Eva. We will have to wait and see."

Johann wrapped his arms around his wife and held her close.

"Remember we are blessed to have arrived safely, Eva, and now begins the adventure."

The following morning dawned with the song of native birds, unfamiliar yet pleasing to the ear. Hope stirred again within the hearts of the settlers as they walked the beach and took in the beauty Langlois had promised them. Tall trees to build houses and a harbour calm and beautiful, a place they knew they would soon call home.

Captains Lavaud, Langlois and Stanley had much to discuss. The problems for the French and the British were now twofold: one of land ownership, the other of governance.

Unfortunately, Maori were prone to sell land to more than one buyer. After Langlois left New Zealand to make arrangements with King Louis Philippe I, the land he had purchased was resold to an English farmer.

A meeting was called with the local tribal chiefs to make another arrangement over the land, although not without difficulty.

Misunderstandings arose due to a lack of knowledge of both language and culture. Maori believed they sold the right to use the land not to own it, a belief that caused trouble in New Zealand on more than one occasion.

Eventually another agreement was signed, similar to that agreed in August 1838 between the tribes and Langlois, and now again two days prior at Pigeon Bay, securing the land for the Nanto-Bordelaise Company.

Governance was a more complicated issue to resolve with differing values and expectations coming into play from all factions. The French were to become divided on this matter.

Lavaud's desire was to claim sovereignty, but to avoid bloodshed until he had heard from his King. Belligny was working for the Nanto-Bordelaise Company, who wanted to develop the settlement under French rule as quickly as possible. He had a dual interest, being also a shareholder in the company.

Langlois was in a quandary. He had given up his land in return for shares in the company, but his greater loyalty was to his passengers to whom he had promised so much. The settlers had little loyalty to the

King or the company, intent as they were on leaving the monarchy and the class system behind. Disappointingly the very situation the settlers were trying to escape had travelled with them to this new land.

British interests were served by Captain Stanley of the *Britomart* and the magistrate Robinson, who were under orders to secure the island for Britain and to keep the peace with Maori whose signatures they wanted on the Treaty of Waitangi.

The Marist priests also had an interest in the outcome, hoping for French rule so that they could carry on their missionary work unimpeded. Pompallier had encouraged Jean-Etienne Pezant to travel with Lavaud on the *Aube* to Akaroa. He knew how the British had used missionary and commercial activity along with land purchases to speed colonisation. Now the French were following that example to smooth the path to French sovereignty.

Jean Pompallier came to visit soon after the renewed land deal had been made, to baptise the baby Libeau who had been born aboard the ship, and to minister to the settlers. In this picture of pride, power and wealth, the priests could see the settlers were being ignored. They needed to work in the background, not wanting to be seen taking sides, encouraging a stand to be made for French rule.

The settlers were determined to leave the politics of France behind and marched in protest, reminding the negotiators they had sailed to New Zealand to be free men, and they wanted to set up a town that gave them this freedom. This was greeted with anger from Lavaud, Belligny and Robinson, none of them wanting to be dictated to by common farmers, gardeners and bakers.

So this trio of powerful men from two countries, used to lording it over those with no ability to fight back, ignored the settlers and continued with their plans. The settlement was to become British, averting at the least the risk of a French penal colony being set up in this beautiful area.

Robinson, the magistrate, was able to speak their language, and set down laws that suited the French. Belligny worked with him to encourage unity between the passengers from the *Comte de Paris* and the increasing numbers of English settlers.

The French settlers were reminded of their contract with the Nanto-Bordelaise Company. They would have to work extremely hard to get the land producing and be self-reliant within eighteen months. This responsibility took precedence over any potential battle for rulership outside of their influence.

Lavaud chose the site for the colonists and by 23rd August the land was marked out into blocks in both

Akarora and Takamatua Bay. The Breitmeyer family volunteered to settle in Takamatua Bay and six of the single German men followed them. The skills of farmers, a sawyer, a carpenter, a baker cum locksmith and a shoemaker were therefore among those that would help this settlement prosper.

The German settlers built a long shed out of timber and covered it with the rushes cleared from the land. This was to be home for them all for the first winter.

Katerina, Elizabeth and their two brothers, Johann and George, didn't care whether the British or French ruled the land.

The work of clearing and planting began. The soil was good and the gardens thrived. Before long, the Breitmeyer family had flowers blooming among the vegetables. Through the long days of labour they kept in mind that soon they would have land to call their own.

At night they laughed and reminisced about the hardships they had been through. They talked about the people left in the homeland that they might never see again, but they never regretted their decision to emigrate.

Sawyers were in demand, especially in German Bay where timber was cut for supplying the entire area. The French settlers built temporary houses at first to get them through the months ahead, mostly without glass in the windows or proper doors.

Once the land was cleared and they were producing food, the temporary houses were replaced ready for the following winter.

Most of the animals did not survive the difficult voyage. Replacements were scarce and the cost of purchasing more at this early stage was prohibitive. The settlers caught fish from the ocean and traded vegetables with Maori for pigeon and weka. Joseph Libeau had brought his own seeds and grapevines with him and, once established, the grapes could be used to make wine, a valuable trading commodity.

While the French settlers busied themselves with wine, the Germans began to make butter and cheese from goats brought in to provide milk. The surplus was traded with the many ships that visited the harbour.

Several more French naval vessels had been sent to protect and assist the settlers as they established their homes. American and French whaling ships were also pleased to trade flour, sugar, rum and tobacco for potatoes, vegetables, wine and cheese.

After only two years wheat was being exported to Sydney and little businesses began to flourish in the now thriving township. Johann Breitmeyer made shoes and boots, teaching his son the trade. The locksmith, baker and hoteliers also contributed.

A track from Takamatua Bay, or German Bay as it

became known, to Akaroa was formed with the assistance of the crews of the *Aube* and the *Comte de Paris.* The German settlers often visited the French settlement, dancing and singing along the path over the hill.

So it was that both communities became an essential part of the development of Banks Peninsula. Johann and Eva gave their children the life they had dared to dream of, with a comfortable home overlooking a bay that would match any in the world for beauty, and an abundance of food.

Chapter 14

Otley, a village in Yorkshire, 1840

John Pawson was a man who craved adventure and right now he had itchy feet. He wanted to do something different, something to better himself. His ancestors had lived in the little town of Otley for generations and now was the time for change.

"I want to do something brave, Maryann. Something that will transform our lives and open the children's minds."

Maryann was a strong and capable woman, with an honest, open face, the sort of person people trusted. A midwife with five children to raise, she was naturally wary of making any sweeping changes.

"Moving to New Zealand where we may be eaten by savages is certainly brave. I am not sure it would change our lives for the better!"

John was quick to respond.

"It's all talk about the natives," he told his wife.

"From what I have read, the Maori are friendly and happy to trade land for commodities. Immigrants have many things to offer them and the trade is good for everyone."

Maryann knew her skills would be missed in her home town, but midwives would be sought after in a young and developing country. John was a builder and wheelwright, also desirable skills. His adventurous spirit indicated he would probably do well in this colony that Britain had taken such a shine to.

New Zealand was a veritable Garden of Eden, apparently, the soil was volcanic and productive, while the colony's oceans were teeming with many kinds of fish.

The Pawson children, William, who was eleven; his eight-year old sister Sara, and the twin six-year olds, John and Jonas, were all excited at the thought of travelling for many months on a ship to a faraway land. Joseph was only one year old, but he joined in with rowdy approval without having any idea of the hardship his parents were embarking upon.

The family were supposed to sail on the *Bolton*, but one child went down with whooping cough. This made it impossible to travel and delayed their trip for a year. The children were that much older, and by now Maryann was pregnant with her sixth child. Of the forty-four passengers to board the ship *Coromandel*, seven were the Pawson family.

The ship was under the command of Captain French, and the ship's surgeon was Dr Alston. The *Coromandel* sailed from St Katherine's Dock, London, at four o'clock on 10th December 1839, and arrived in Wellington on 29th August 1840. But not before it had docked in Sydney, spending some time there before picking up two hundred sheep, forty bullocks and four horses bound for the farms of New Zealand.

The journey was not easy for anyone on board, but more difficult for John and Maryann, whose little boy Edwin was stillborn six weeks into the trip. All the passengers stood on the deck beside the tiny body covered by the Union Jack flag. Many shed tears for the parents and siblings of this lost child who would never know the life his parent had planned for him. A fellow passenger played *Amazing Grace* on his fiddle.

Maryann sang the words softly in a vain attempt to ease the heartache as the little bundle slid into the dark and forbidding ocean.

The time spent in Sydney, with its broad roads and busy throngs crowding well-established shops, did nothing to prepare the passengers for what they saw when they landed in the town of Wellington. The colonists lived in tents or small whare that did little to protect them from the incessant rain and cold that a New Zealand August can bring.

Grog shops had sprung up along the shore, making liquor easy to buy. The local Maori tended to become unruly after consuming too much of the strong drink and that caused concern among the newcomers.

Maryann soon found a friend in Lizzy Brown, who had arrived six months before the Pawson family. Peter and Lizzy had travelled from Scotland on the *Bengal Merchant*.

Lizzy lived in terror of the Maori. On one occasion she had found herself caught up in a street skirmish that ended in her being chased along the street by a native wielding a tomahawk.

The Browns had bought land on the banks of the Hutt River. Lizzy's fears were heightened when she had to cross a flooded stream, while natives clustering on the bank yelled that the 'taipo' (evil spirit) would seize her. Maryann was quick to point out to her husband John that Maori were not as friendly as he had depicted them.

Maryann was on hand when Lizzy's baby was due to be born. Baby Peter was the first white child to be born in the Hutt Valley. The delivery was not without incident, however, because the river overflowed its banks and the bed where Lizzy lay began to float. It was impossible to move her and there was talk of suspending the mattress from the rafters of the whare.

Lizzy stood her ground. She reminded them, "the whare is only built from scrub tied together with flax. It will probably collapse. I do not wish to be swept away down the river with a baby in my arms. We'll wait it out."

She chose wisely. The river went down over night.

The road from Wellington to Petone and Lower Hut was one of the first undertakings by the early settlers, and it was a man called Sam Phelps who made the first trip with his bullock and dray. He started a regular coach service, where goods were moved by bullock and dray, and even donkeys were put to work.

The first donkeys to arrive by ship were to be a source of great amusement to Maori because of the big ears. Maori nicknamed them 'rabbiti nui' meaning big rabbit.

John and Maryann were expecting another child and their first baby to be born in New Zealand arrived in February, 1842, and named Edwin after his brother who did not survive the long journey.

The year Edwin was born was the year of the big fire on Lambton Quay. As he grew up Edwin heard the story many times of how forty buildings were totally destroyed after embers from open cooking fires were scattered across the town by the brisk winds. His parents taught him how sad and disappointed the settlers were to see so many buildings burn down. Some would have liked to return to their homes in Europe but they did not have enough money

The friendship between the Pawsons and the Browns was cemented by the arrival of the two new babies, and together the families began to carve out a future in New Zealand. Word spread north of a settlement of French and German immigrants doing well in Akaroa on Banks Peninsula.

The Browns, who were already expecting another child, decided a quieter life would suit them better. The close friendship between the Browns and the Pawsons was interrupted when the Browns set sail on the schooner *Scotia* for Akaroa. The winds battered the little vessel and it took two weeks to reach their destination, but the sight that met the Browns on their arrival was one they would never forget.

The bush was lush, and the sweetest of songs from the tui could be heard proclaiming the bush to be theirs. The harbour was long and calm, dotted with whaling vessels. Patches of land had been cleared by the French settlers to grow grape vines, fruit and walnut trees.

Willows dipped their branches into a stream. The cuttings were from willows on the island of St Helena where General Napoleon Bonaparte had been exiled. This was where the Browns could be truly happy, a quiet settlement where families worked together to build a country they could be proud of.

Six months after they moved, a girl child Elizabeth was born in a tiny cottage in the centre of town where in later years Bruce Green would build a hotel. The Browns kept in touch with John and Maryann, letting them know how quickly the area was growing. They explained how the bush needed clearing to build more substantial homes for both the French and the increasing number of British folk who were beginning to move there.

John had joined the police force in Wellington, but was ready for a change, and he and Maryann were drawn to join their friends in this prosperous region.

"We would do well to build a mill in Akaroa, Maryann. There is plenty of timber and each year more and more settlers will be moving to the Canterbury region."

"A good idea," Maryann agreed, "and the growing population means there will always be babies to deliver."

By 1850 the Pawsons were reunited with their friends, joining the sixty French, twenty German and a growing number of British settlers. There were also around one hundred Maori who were of a much friendlier disposition than the Browns and Pawsons had experienced in the North Island.

The local tribes played an important role in trading food to both the settlers and the many whaling ships that anchored in the bay.

John was happy.

"This is the adventure we were looking for, this is the land of plenty, we have good soil to grow pasture and there will be work in cutting down the forest for many years to come."

"There is beauty here to rival our home in Yorkshire," agreed Maryann. "The people are welcoming and warm-hearted. Our children will experience a diverse culture, unlike what they could expect in Otley."

John set up his mill and the Pawsons quickly settled in to life in and around Akaroa. He had his eye on some fine trees in Duvauchelle Bay, named after two brothers who owned land but never lived there. Duvauchelle and the nearby settlement, Head of Bay, were across the water from Akaroa and German Bay.

The first white man to settle in Duvauchelle was Joseph Libeau who had arrived on the *Comte de Paris* with his wife Madeleine and their three children. Libeau caught a whaling ship across to the bay and one year later built a whare.

His son, the same young Joseph who had lost his cap after the storm on the boat coming to New Zealand, grew up to be an adventurous lad who tried his hand at working on a cutter up the Yarra River in Melbourne.

On his travels around Australia, young Joseph sailed to Hobart where he was horrified by the number of convicts with shaved heads in chains, working on bridges and civic buildings. He was pleased indeed to work his passage back to the French settlement and marry Clemence Rose Glendrot who had sailed on the *Comte de Paris* with him. Joseph built a house for Clemence on the same land as his parents, that measured twenty-four feet by twelve feet, and they lived there for the rest of their lives.

The hills above Duvauchelle and Head of Bay were rich in mature totara and black pine. The totara trees were tall and straight with vast girths; one was measured with a circumference of sixty-six feet. John travelled from German Bay to the area to cut timber periodically, but did not live there until 1857 when he bought a mill from Mr Bryant in Barry's Bay, renaming it York Mill after his home county.

One of John's early contracts was to cut the timber for the Hotel de Pècheurs in Duvauchelle for the builders, Messrs Tribe and Selig. The hotel was built in 1851 for one of the French settlers, Francois Le Lievre. Francois, an original settler off the *Comte de Paris* was an enterprising man who also ran a ferry service to Lyttelton Harbour. This saved travellers tramping over the hills, which was a hard journey along tracks formed by Maori.

This was a community built almost entirely on the timber industry, milling trees for timber, firewood and the important shipbuilding industry. Men worked hard, long hours to cut millions of tons of timber to build houses in Akaroa and the now developing Canterbury area. Boat builders supplied ships for local use as well as to ports all over New Zealand.

The timber industry was booming. John Pawson's free spirit soon had him looking for the next venture. He saw the value of owning the Duvauchelle Hotel and promptly purchased it. The men employed in his mills would gather in the bar after a hard day's work to spend their well-earned wages on a cool beer or two to ease dry throats.

Akaroa grew, the population grew and the children grew. The Browns from Scotland, the Pawsons from Yorkshire and the Breitmeyers from Kandel, along with the many other families, could narrate interesting tales of lands far away. All had taken the brave step of emigrating to the farthest land. Few were sad to be here where there was food for all and business was booming.

Chapter 15

The next generation. 1855
John and Maryann Pawson's daughter Sara Pawson grew up and began a whirlwind romance with James George Stevenson who had arrived in Akaroa a year before. He had left his home in Kent, England, departing for Auckland, but the ship *Balnagileth* ran out of provisions and was forced to dock in Lyttelton.

Sara was at once smitten by the newcomer, a handsome man with a neatly trimmed beard, who could turn his hand to any work on the land.

Sara was ready to fly the nest and make a life of her own and neither were surprised when Sara became pregnant. The shame brought to bear on women who conceived out of wedlock in those days should not be underestimated. A church wedding was out of the question, and there were many who would point the finger, whispering cruel gossip.

James and Sara refused to let such scandalmongers

pursue them in this new land. Instead, they held their heads high and planned a marriage ceremony at the courthouse. James was a clever man who understood Akaroa and Canterbury would prove to be a prosperous area to settle.

He trusted Sara to support him, and, in return, was happy to love and care for her for as long as they both should live.

Sara's brother William proposed to his childhood sweetheart, Katerina Breitmeyer. Katerina and her sister Elizabeth had followed the Pawson boys everywhere when they were growing up. William knew from the time Katerina turned fifteen that she was the girl for him. She had developed into a kind, beautiful and loving young woman.

Wanting to be sure she was old enough to know her own mind, he waited five more years until her twentieth birthday to ask her to marry him.

The couple had been celebrating Katerina's birthday in Akaroa, and walked back over the hill track to German Bay. The night was warm and the sea was as smooth as glass, mirroring the trees along the shoreline.

William took Katerina's hand and led her to the sand dunes where they could sit and look out over the water. Lights flickered in the cabin windows of ships anchored in the bay, and reflected on the calm water.

"How lucky we are to be here," murmured Katerina. "How lucky that our parents were brave enough to come to New Zealand."

"If they hadn't, we'd never have met."

William drew his pretty fräulein closer, and touched her chin so that she turned to face him.

"I want you to be my wife, Katerina. I've known you most of my life and I know I'll never love anyone like I love you. Will you marry me?"

William was always direct; not a man who believed in frills or small talk. He knew what he wanted, and now he'd finally admitted he wanted her.

Katerina laughed softly. Laying back on the sand, she pulled William down beside her and pressed her mouth to his. The surge of longing that came with his kiss confirmed for her that saying yes was the right decision.

When they finally drew apart, she whispered, "I will be happy to be your wife, William."

"We could get married on the same day as Sara if you can sew your dress in time. There will be time to read the banns if I speak with your father tomorrow."

Katerina understood the special bond between William and his sister Sara. She shared the same kind of closeness with her own sister Elizabeth, and with her brothers George and Johann. All had been children travelling together to an unfamiliar and magical land.

Here they had learned different languages and forged a culture that was a mixture of their homeland traditions and new customs better suited to New Zealand life.

A joint wedding would be a happy day for both the families. Like all young women Katerina had gathered up a trousseau, and agreed she could be ready in time. They had both waited long enough and could easily arrange their own wedding to coincide with the civil ceremony for Sara and James.

William, who had been patient for a long time now, was both relieved and excited that Katerina was so ready to commit to him. This moment was a dream come true. His hold tightened as he ran a hand down the softness of her breast, thrilled when she responded to his caress. As suppressed passion welled up in him, he dared to slide his hand beneath her long skirt and petticoat and stroke her warm, smooth thighs.

Katerina could not deny her response, but wasn't yet ready to yield. She wanted them to wait until they were joined as man and wife. Gently she withdrew herself from William's hold and, biting her lip, she asked him to be patient a little longer.

"The wedding night will be here before we know it William, in the meantime we have the distraction of making wedding plans."

Traditionally, there were three stages to a German wedding. Firstly, the civil ceremony known as the 'Standesbeamte', which was followed by 'Plolterabend,' the evening of broken porcelain, an important ritual to ensure happiness and good luck. Friends and family would bring old kitchenware to smash in front of the bride and groom, who were left to clean it up as a lesson in co-operation. Thirdly, the religious ceremony, which was when the bride wore her white gown and veil.

The wedding preparations brought much excitement not only to the Pawsons and Breitmeyers, but also to the Browns and other families in Akaroa and German Bay. This would be a grand celebration with much rejoicing.

The two couples were married in the Registry Office, Sara's waist swollen with the love-child due in three months. The Plolterabend was held on the evening before guests gathered at the Anglican Church to see Katerina and William joined in holy matrimony.

The reception was the very best the German, French, English and Scottish guests could have imagined. Speeches for both couples brought tears and laughter. After the formal celebrations, the party was open to anyone who wanted to join in. Peter

Brown played his bagpipes, the sound drawing folk from all around.

Maori had a soft spot for the Scottish settlers and answered the call of the pipes, dressed in flax skirts decorated with intricate designs and cloaks threaded with exotic feathers. Their women danced with poi, swaying gracefully and fluttering their hands, telling the story of the arrival of the settlers from across the sea, and the joining in love of the young couples. There were Scottish dancers in kilts, German dancers in traditional costumes, all songs and dances a blend of cultures and customs.

This was the first generation to wed and make families of their own in German Bay. Only three months to wait for Sara's baby to be born and baptised John Edward Stevenson. He brought those blessings only a baby can bring to the grandparents, and to the community in general.

William and Katerina's first baby Amelia, conceived on their wedding night, was born in February the following year. Her arrival signalled that two families from different backgrounds who had gone through hardship to make a better life for future generations were now joined and pleased to be so.

Two years later, in 1857, William's brother, John Pawson pledged his love to Katerina's sister, Elizabeth, whom he married in March. By now both Sara and

Katerina were expecting their second babies. Sara's Mary, named after her grandmother Maryann Pawson, was born on 23rd July, and Katerina's Ellen four days later. Two cousins who became as close as twins, growing up to share childhood and teenage adventures.

By 1862 Elizabeth Brown was old enough to marry Katerina and Elizabeth's brother, George Breitmeyer. The thirteen offspring of this union would fuse the Scottish blood of the Browns to the Germanic Breitmeyers. The Pawsons, Browns and Breitmeyers were united as close families spreading far and wide across New Zealand. Cousins hearing the stories of parents and grandparents about the long journeys across the sea to a better land.

William, John and Jonas Pawson followed their father into the milling business, setting up their own mill further up the valley near where William was building a house for himself and Katerina. The family took part in the rapid deforestation of the Banks Peninsula.

The terrain was steep so not all the trees could be milled, but there was plenty of timber for the ever-increasing demand for wood to build houses in both the peninsula and the fast-growing Christchurch region. The mechanised mills used first water then steam, allowing work to proceed at a greater speed than earlier when sawyers worked by hand in pits at the head of the various bays.

By 1863 a new steam mill was built capable of turning out 12,000 feet of timber a week. Wood as fuel was in demand, especially in Canterbury, where at times the demand was greater than for sawn timber.

1855 also heralded the beginning of democracy in New Zealand, even though it was the second election to be held. The first election in 1853 was held when the colony was still part of the British Empire. To qualify as a voter in that election one needed to be male, a British subject aged twenty-one or older, and a land owner. Only some ten thousand votes were cast.

Harry Sewell, regarded as the first premier, campaigned for self-government and New Zealand's separation from the Empire. The first Parliament did not have the ability to appoint a Cabinet, but the 1855 Parliament gained that power, so that was the election which heralded the beginning of democracy.

In the early elections, all candidates were independent and Governments were formed on loose coalitions. This meant no one could claim they had won an election. It was up to the Prime Minister to make deals with as many independent members as possible to get his policies accepted.

John Cuff was elected to represent Akaroa and the new government assisted the locals by granting one hundred pounds towards a road to open up Head of Bay. John Pawson was voted onto the Roads Committee, and William cut the first road from the Bay to a settlement on the coast named Little Akaloa.

As roads improved and more settlers arrived, there was a tendency to burn off the forest, especially on the higher hills. This reflected a general urgency towards increasing pastureland, a trend to make this country more like the land they had left behind.

With these changes came unwanted fires spreading from burn-offs and carelessness at the mills resulting in many lost acres. Such wastefulness contributed to the decimation of the forests earlier than anticipated.

Yet the burning of the forest also spawned the next successful industry for the peninsula: the growing of cocksfoot seed. The seed had been brought from Europe and was found to be the best grass to sow over the ashes of the burnt-out areas. On top of this, Canterbury had begun the farming of Merino sheep because of their fine quality wool. The farmers needed a strong healthy grass to feed the stock.

The seed became known as Akaroa cocksfoot and was sold both locally and exported to Australia.

Chapter 16

Goldrush, 1862

John Pawson was on the look-out for a new project. Maybe it was the lure of riches, but more likely the search for adventure that drove him to announce he would join the search for gold at Gabriel's Gully, Otago.

He disregarded pleas not to go from his wife and family, assuring them he could look after himself and painting a word picture of the wealth he intended to bring back. Wealth that would change the fortunes of all his family for generations to come. His enthusiasm was catching and before long both John and his good friend Peter Brown were making their way to the goldfields.

Gold had been discovered in June 1861. Over the next six months the news spread, and Dunedin was inundated with some fourteen thousand people, increasing the population many times over. The face of Otago was to be changed forever.

John and Peter were well-organised for their adventure with money enough to buy the necessary equipment to get them started on their eight square metre claim. The work was difficult, using picks to loosen the hard ground before shovelling the gravelly soil into sluice pans. For hours they stood, swirling the cold water through the soil, encouraging the gold to settle in the bottom of the pans, sometimes nothing but gleaming specks, at other times nice-sized nuggets.

All were carefully wrapped and stored in a hiding place until they could be weighed and sold for cash. There was much talk in the fields of the gold rushes in California and Victoria, and such stories of success kept them working long and tiring days, hoping for that big break. John Pawson and Peter Brown were part of what was to be the first of three major gold rushes throughout New Zealand.

The winter of 1862 brought savage weather that caused many to leave the fields for the comforts of home, but something much worse was to beset the goldfields.

Along with the many hard-working men who supported each other in the fields, there were those who had no scruples; some from the goldfields of Australia, bitter and disillusioned; others ex-convicts who had served their time in Norfolk and Van Diemen's Land and wanted to claw back the lost years.

A few were wicked men who wanted to profit from the effort of others, and it was men like this who changed the lives of the Pawsons, the Browns and the Breitmeyers forever.

The night was bleak, with a heavy rain earlier and the howling wind drowning out sounds in the darkness. John woke with a start in the early hours of the morning and fumbled to light the lamp, becoming aware of scuffling and swearing some distance from the tent. Peter had gone.

John lifted the tent flap and waited for his eyes to adjust. In the meagre light, he saw four men standing and staring down at a shape on the ground.

John lifted his lamp to see what the men were so interested in. He saw Peter, curled up on the ground, silent and unmoving. The men stopped arguing and turned their attention to John. Realisation dawned on him that they had been up to no good and Peter had disturbed them.

The intruders were faced with the inescapable truth they had killed a man.

"We'll have to take him down. We got nothin' more t' lose."

John armed himself with a shovel, the only weapon near to hand. He was a strong man, a builder and sawyer who all his life had done heavy work. Still he was no match for these savage and determined criminals, who would not stop at killing the man who had witnessed their grisly crime.

Swiftly the men surrounded him, lashing out with sticks and metal pipes, taking turns to move in, evading the shovel swung desperately by John to keep them at bay.

Eventually he lost his footing on the wet ground. Like dogs at a kill, the men moved in, beating and kicking him until John at last lay still.

The three families that would grieve for John Pawson and Peter Brown never found out who was behind the violent deaths. The case was lost in a backlog of police files and remains a mystery to this day. The bereaved families would join other wives and children left without husbands and fathers.

John's son William fell ill with fever when he heard the news. His grieving mother visited to tend him, sponging him down and giving him willow bark to chew to reduce his temperature.

"Keep water available for him to drink," Maryann instructed her daughter-in-law Katerina. "Keep sponging him down. I will check on him tomorrow."

Peter's daughter Elizabeth and her husband George were awaiting the birth of his first grandchild. Lizzy Brown asked her good friend Maryann to call on the young couple, to prescribe a calming draught for Elizabeth until the baby came. The two widows were once again drawn together for a birth, this time with the deeply painful loss of loved ones searing their hearts.

The gold rush changed New Zealand, and the stories that came from the goldfields were not always good. The population grew faster than the resources, and unsolved crimes were not uncommon. Otago's population escalated eighty percent during the first four years of the discovery of gold. The settlement had increased by forty-thousand up until the 1860s. In the next twenty years, nearly five hundred thousand Europeans found their way there.

The early population growth included ex-convicts from both Norfolk Island and Van Diemen's Land, some arriving as early as 1837. The government had been naive in believing New Zealand to be a community of purer origin than Australia. Numbers ranging from two to three hundred former convicts now lived and worked amongst the immigrants, not to mention deserting sailors and escaped prisoners eager to begin anew.

Immigration followed its own demographics and included a colourful and interesting mixture of race, class and moral codes. Among the former prisoners to make their way to Akaroa in 1859 was Ben Shadbolt, one of the four men transported to Norfolk Island from Datchworth. Ben had served twelve years of his sentence, four months of hard labour, and three of those in irons.

By 1848 Solomon, George, John and Ben Shadbolt had been transferred from Norfolk Island to Van Diemen's Land and put to work on government projects building bridges and houses. This is where Solomon died after surviving the harsh years on Norfolk Island. The younger men were left to work out their time without him. His son George, sobered by his father's death, settled down and did not offend again, choosing a life befitting his conversion to the Methodist religion.

John threatened to burn down his employer's house, and was sentenced to another four months' hard labour, serving his time on the opposite side of the island. His brother Ben managed to get himself into trouble stealing geese from his employer, and then stepped up to horse theft, an understandable scenario given his love of horses.

By now Ben had met an ex-convict called Elizabeth, who was to become his second great love. He had stolen the horse to visit her, but in turn ended up with three months' hard labour in Port Arthur. The long-suffering Elizabeth was left to struggle on her own with the three children Ben had fathered.

When Ben could finally call himself a free man, his thoughts turned to the nearby country of New Zealand. There he could throw off the label of convict and start anew. John had moved on to try his luck in the Victorian goldfields and cousin George was determined to make his home in Van Diemen's Land, regardless of the stigma he would carry as an ex-convict. He opened a wheelwright workshop and became a successful businessman.

The trip to New Zealand turned into a nightmare for Ben and his family. The weather crossing the Tasman was so bad the ship was forced to turn back.

Many, including Ben's oldest child Linden, suffered from extreme mal de mer. He was so ill that his mother Elizabeth refused to take the boy on the ship when it sailed for the second time, and Ben made a decision that would haunt him for the rest of his life.

He left the boy with his cousin George. Abandoning a child for the second time added to the deep grief within caused by leaving Carolyn to raise Clara in Datchworth. Linden did not know his father well because Ben had spent much of his son's life in prison. It was a relief for him to stay with the uncle he knew better and not ever have to board a ship again if he didn't want to.

Ben kept in touch with a group of ex-convicts he had known in Van Diemen's Land, and soon after his arrival in Akaroa he left Elizabeth with the children and sailed to Wellington to a business meeting. The meeting was profitable for all concerned and from that day Ben lived an exemplary life on the spoils he believed the Australian and British governments owed him.

New Zealand offered a chance for Ben and Elizabeth and their two girls, Emma and Amelia, to live the life they had always dreamed of. The family soon made a favourable impression on the growing community of Akaroa, passing themselves off as immigrants of noble background who had arrived via Australia. Ben was welcomed onto various committees with the Pawsons, Browns and other early settlers.

Ben became a trustee of John's York Mill company and eventually bought the mill after John's tragic death.

Chapter 17

Ben and Elizabeth Shadbolt prospered. They managed to keep their past a secret, and became well-respected members of the community.

The couple were of a sociable disposition, and when Anderson's Accommodation House, formerly the Duvauchelle Hotel owned by John Pawson, came up for sale, they saw its purchase as a great opportunity. Elizabeth put her heart and soul into the venture, renaming the hotel 'The Travellers Rest' and making it an important centre for the community to gather.

Ironically because of the fear of unruly behaviour from patrons in the Bay, one condition of the liquor licence was for the patron to be sworn in as the local constable. So it was that the ex-convict, unbeknown to the authorities, was to become the law.

Ben dabbled in many ventures: milling, farming and horse breeding. His skill with horses, and the talent to recognise a winner, led to him becoming highly regarded as a breeder of racehorses. A shipping service to carry mail and passengers from settlement to settlement around the bays was a good adjunct to his sawmilling business, making it easy for workers to travel to the work sites.

Ben could also see the advantage in dairy farming in Akaroa now that the land was cleared and the cocksfoot grass growing well. He contacted his brother Peter in Datchworth and offered to assist with the purchase of a farm on Banks Peninsula. This was his opportunity to repay Peter for what he had done for the family left behind to fend for themselves.

Peter, the quieter of the brothers, had always believed in the future of the dairy industry. His great desire to own a dairy farm could now become a reality if the family moved to New Zealand.

Peter's wife, Ann, had one concern.

"How can we take seven children all that way? We won't be able to look after them on a ship; they'll be all over the place. The twins are only five months old and still need constant care."

"Mary Ann, Jonathan and Frederick are old enough to help mind Emily, and William. They can help us and we'll look after a twin each. Peter and Sarah will hardly notice they aren't at home."

"What if they get seasick? What if I get seasick?"

"It won't last. The young get their sea-legs quickly. Ann, this is our big opportunity and we should make the most of it. We will be able to get the farm we have dreamed of. I've checked the shipping lines and the *British Empire* is a sturdy ship and has been completely overhauled. It's not like the early days of sailing; things have improved a great deal since then."

What Peter didn't know is why the *British Empire* had been overhauled. She was an unlucky ship, christened the *Demerara*. On one occasion she had got wedged across a river with her bow stuck in a mud bank on one side and her stern in the riverbank on the other. She was stranded so high at low tide that smaller vessels sailed beneath her, undignified for any ship. The stranding caused major damage to her structure so she was repaired and renamed.

This did not change the ship's luck. In fact, each subsequent sailing brought a different commander and yet another calamity.

By 15th May 1864, when Peter and his family were ready to sail, it was Captain Callenan who took the helm, but not until he had supervised the rebuilding of her deck, still misshapen after the stranding on the riverbank. Peter and Ann shared the voyage with thirty-three saloon passengers and three hundred and sixty-six immigrants.

Two passengers of note were a Mr Prince, who had

brought with him a variety of English birds that his servant Thomas was instructed to care for. Not an easy task on a sailing ship, trying to refill water containers and feed bowls. Alas, by the end of the journey many of the birds had escaped to a watery death.

The other, a Mr Johnson, had built a mysterious container on the quarter deck, which he later explained held fish to fill New Zealand's welcoming rivers. He had brought mostly trout, perch and carp, with a few tench, royal-rudd, roach and goldfish. In addition, there were various weeds as a food source and to purify the water.

Fortunately, none but a few goldfish survived, and the ship's newspaper reported a 'lump of white putty' was found in the tank, apparently causing the fish to die.

The surgeon aboard was Andrew Nash, a man with an optimistic outlook who felt that the loss of ten babies to diarrhoea was not a bad effort, considering there were forty infants under one year old on board when the *British Empire* set sail.

A twenty-five percent loss seems a high price to pay even in those far-off days, and would certainly have been reason enough not to travel if Ann had been forewarned.

There were five adult deaths, three of whom, in the

doctor's words, were either decrepit or in delicate health on boarding. The other two were fine young men who died of fever in the tropics.

The word 'sacrifice' comes to mind. Did these families know there was one chance in four their baby would not make it to their destination?

There were five births on the ship, though one newborn to a young couple died five days later. The ship's fortunes had not changed, this time doomed with the loss of so many young lives.

The percentage of loss was slightly higher because, although all of the Shadbolt children arrived in New Zealand, one of the twins, Peter, died seven days after reaching Lyttelton. This was the result of prolonged diarrhoea and difficulty in keeping food down while aboard ship

Peter junior was only ten months old when he succumbed. He had met his cousins, even though he was so poorly; but this was not the family reunion so eagerly looked forward to. Instead of joy and laughter, Peter and Ann's life in New Zealand had begun with immeasurable sadness.

Ben, Elizabeth and their family and friends gathered around to give support. Maryann Pawson was called in to rally the little boy, but it was too late; there was nothing she could do. Little Peter's new life in Akaroa with his cousins was not to be.

After the funeral, the family gathered together to express a range of feelings from joy to sadness. The cousins Mary, Jonathan and Frederick talked with their New Zealand cousins about the home and family they had left behind in England.

Ben spoke of his son Linden in Van Diemen's Land, now renamed Tasmania.

"Twelve years old now, the same age as you, lad," he said ruffling young Frederick's hair.

Peter's eldest, Mary Ann, spoke of her recent marriage to Hugh Dalgleish and of Clara, who had been her bridesmaid.

"You saw Clara often?"

Ben had a lump in his throat and his blue eyes shone with tears as he asked the question.

"We rode the ponies together, and I liked to visit her in the big house with Aunt Carolyn. Especially after church on Sundays when old Mrs Ellis cooked special food with dessert and everything."

"Clara's mother was a superb horsewoman," mused Ben. "It sounds like Clara took after her."

"Oh, yes. Clara always left me behind. She could ride like the wind."

"You'll have plenty of horse riding here. We always need riders to exercise the horses."

When the women and children had grown silent from the overwhelming fatigue of the day, Elizabeth suggest they get some well-earned rest, then went to bed herself.

Ben and Peter had years to catch up on. Ben poured a drink for his brother.

"Tell me of Carolyn."

"The transportation was hard on all the women, Ben, but Carolyn came off the worst. She raised a fine daughter in Clara, but she was unable to have more children to take her mind off things. She was fond of Edward Cole; he was a good man and gave her security and some happiness, but it wasn't enough. The wound was too deep. There was always something missing in her life, a craving that could not be fulfilled. The joy she'd known when you were both young was gone.:

"Ann and I watched, helpless, as her health deteriorated. Nothing, it seemed, could pull her out of it. When Clara was sixteen she left home and moved to Surrey, south of London. She was happy there, near her Great Aunt Eleanor, Aunt Jemima and her cousins."

"From that time on Carolyn gave in to her illness and slipped from our grasp. Even Edward couldn't help her, though he never stopped loving Carolyn with all his heart. She was only thirty-five, too young for a woman of such beauty and strength to perish."

Ben had never fully recovered from his forced

abandonment of Carolyn and his unborn baby Clara. Now he was flooded with sadness and the worst of all emotions – remorse – on hearing how his beloved first wife had withered away. He should have been there to love and protect her. Carolyn, who had often told him he was capable of achieving great things, had never known or shared in his success. She would never be here to stroke the necks of his elegant mares and priceless stallions, to ride the horses along the beaches and help to train them for the race track.

Ben's grief was somewhat eased in his close relationship with his daughters by Elizabeth. He shared a particular bond with Amelia because of her love of horses. As with Carolyn so long ago, Ben valued her opinion and kept her by his side, teaching her about his business dealings, and riding together. She was his constant companion.

The weeks following the baby's funeral were busy for Peter and Ann. They needed a property with a house big enough to accommodate a family of six children ranging from eighteen years to one. They bought property in Robinson's Bay around the harbour from Duvauchelle towards Akaroa, a fine piece of land for a dairy herd, with access to the creamery.

☆

Peter and Ann's family brought new blood into the region and they continued to add to the population with five more children born in New Zealand. Life was hard but rewarding, with the children to help with the milking and running the farm. They made friends readily and enjoyed the camaraderie of so many different nationalities, something they had not experienced in England.

The Akaroa area was developing fast, with more and more houses, shops and community centres built over the years. Improved roading meant merchandise could be delivered by horse and cart. Families could travel together in carriages to meetings and to social events.

Boats were still a quicker way to get from one settlement to another, cutting across the water to visit Duvauchelle or around to Akaroa for supplies. It was a sailboat ride to pick up supplies one sunny afternoon that brought further tragedy to Peter and Ann's family, seven years after they had arrived in New Zealand.

In 1871 on Monday 16th April, Mary Ann, her husband Hugh and Emily, now thirteen years old, set off in a small boat to Akaroa for provisions. Another boat left at the same time with friends from Duvauchelle Bay. The group spent the day in town, then in the evening they boarded the boats for the trip home.

The weather was fine when they set off, but that can change quickly in this harbour, with rough weather blowing up in minutes. The group split up, with Mary Ann, Hugh and Emily together in one boat with the skipper and a male friend. The second boat was skippered by John Reed and carried two other friends.

They had not rowed far and were approaching the southernmost point of Lushington Bay, when clouds darkened the sky. Visibility decreased until the passengers could hardly make out each other's faces. The wind whipped up the waves and it was hard work to keep the boats on course. The boat carrying the Shadbolts was getting into trouble.

"Best we change places, lad."

The skipper moved Hugh off the front oar to the bow to keep watch.

"I can't see much," yelled Hugh.

"Do the best you can. I'll keep her off the reef."

The sea was heavy, and seemed determined on destruction. The wind blew harder and rain fell in torrents, flooding the boat. The skipper struggled to hold the boat from heading towards the point, using all his strength and experience to keep afloat.

Then, with a sickening lurch, the bow struck the reef and went down within seconds, stern first, before rolling over with the keel uppermost. The women screamed as they were tipped into the seething water. The skipper tried to cling to the keel, but was washed away and forced to swim for the rocks. It took three attempts before he got some traction and crawled on hands and knees to the shore.

He called as loud as he could and finally located passengers from the second boat, which managed to slide onto the reef without turning over. Though the waves threatened to pull them out to sea, the passengers were able to scramble towards the shore, fighting to reach safety. The survivors called out to the four who were still missing, but their voices were lost in the sounds of the storm.

Half of the friends had made it to safety. There was no sign of the others.

The survivors searched through the night without seeing or hearing anything. One of the skippers eventually walked to German Bay and alerted a farmer, who in turn notified the police. A dawn search at low tide found the two boats on the rocks, no more than a chain apart, one still upside down.

Clothing began to wash ashore, a shawl belonging to Mary Ann, a man's cap and a white petticoat, followed by soap and coffee. Then a body was discovered lying across a rock – Mary Ann, the only one among the four drowned that night whose body was ever recovered.

Mary Ann's husband Hugh, Emily, and the other adults eluded the desperate searchers. The fashion of the day was not conducive to water safety, with clothes soon becoming unbearably heavy, dragging the wearer below the surface.

The news of the tragic losses spread around the peninsula, and it wasn't long before the community were pitching in to help with the funerals. Young Frederick, still only eighteen, was grief stricken. He was meant to be on the boat, but had pulled out at the last minute to meet up with friends.

He believed he could have helped save his young sister Emily if he had been there. The family could not console him, not even his Uncle Ben, who had taken a special shine to Frederick because he was the same age as his cousin Linden in Tasmania.

After the funeral service, the mourners met at The Travellers Rest. Peter and Ann were uplifted by the attendance and support of so many of the community. The mourners included two young women, from German Bay, who were cousins. Mary Stevenson and Ellen Pawson were four years younger than Frederick and acutely aware of Frederick's pain and guilt.

They approached him and spoke words that only the young know how to say to the each other, convincing him he was not responsible for the death of his sister and he should not blame himself. Though Frederick's guilt lingered forever, it was much diminished by the kindness shown to him that day.

Frederick had seen Ellen and Mary on many occasions since he first landed in New Zealand, remembering them because they were such great friends. Full of fun and more like twins than cousins. Now he noticed how grown-up they had become, changing at only fourteen years of age into wise young women.

Mary, he remembered was named after her grandmother, the midwife who had helped when his brother Peter was so sick after the journey to New Zealand. Ellen's father was the midwife's son, and her mother was Katerina, who still spoke with a German accent.

Mary and Ellen kept in touch with Frederick after the funeral, and they became closer as they grew older, mixing with Frederick's cousins Emma and Amelia Shadbolt. Ben's hotel became the ideal place for the young folk to hang-out, with horses to ride and Elizabeth always ready to pamper them with milk and cookies.

The cousins noticed some tension between Frederick and his parents. Peter and Ann were happy with their quiet life and didn't mind being tied down with milking. Frederick wasn't sure he wanted to milk cows and feed calves. The farm and the milking shed was his father's dream, not his. He envied his cousins' freedom.

Frederick's Uncle Ben gave his children almost anything they wanted. They had horses of their own and their father was well-known and influential in the town. Frederick enjoyed the time he spent with his uncle and cousins away from the tasks and ties of the milking shed.

Chapter 18

A new face was seen amongst the men who came to lodge at Ben's hotel. Jack Wallace had moved from Whanganui with his brother Archie and his wife. The brothers opened a business together, Jack as a blacksmith and Archie as a wheelwright.

Word spread that Jack had been a soldier and his family were well-known and respected military men in the Wellington, Whanganui and Taranaki area.

The community welcomed the brothers and Ben gave them work shoeing his horses and mending wagons from the mill. He recommended them to others and the brothers found they had a worthwhile business on their hands. Sometimes Jack and Arthur worked in the sawmills, learning to be sawyers, as well as helping in the cocksfoot fields at harvest time.

Jack was pleased the war had ended. He enjoyed the freedom and the friendships of his new life in the prosperous Banks Peninsula. He particularly liked the pretty young woman called Ellen Pawson who visited the hotel. Ellen enjoyed Jack's company and told him all about her mother Katerina and how she had travelled to New Zealand from Germany on the *Comte de Paris* when she was a child.

"When she grew up, she married her childhood sweetheart, my father William, who sailed from a village in England the same year."

She shared how she and her cousin Mary had been born within four days of each other, and how both had the same grandfather, John Pawson.

"We all loved Grandpa Pawson. He would take us to his mill and let us run down the piles of sawdust. He taught us to ride the ponies and made us aware of our history and where our ancestors had come from. He learned my mother's language and helped me to speak correct English.

"He was an adventurous man and keen to make us all rich. He went to Gabriel's Gully and staked a claim with his good friend, Peter Brown."

Tears welled in Ellen's eyes as she shared this story with Jack.

"When I was nearly eight years old, a constable came to our home. He sat us down in the sitting room where we waited and wondered why he had come – we searched each other's faces hoping for a clue.

"Though I was scared something terrible had

happened, I hung on to the belief that it would be something my parents could fix. At last he explained that my grandpa would not be coming home. When I was older, I learned how the two friends had been attacked and murdered outside their tent."

Jack put his arm around Ellen and let her cry. There was no need to speak; he understood her loss. He thought of his own brother, killed in a land-war in Taranaki, a war that ended with no winners. When Ellen's tears dried, he spoke gently.

"I lost my brother in the battle at Te Ngutu o te mana. One minute they are with us, the next they are gone, and you can no longer talk to them. I do talk to Richard in my mind, but it's not the same."

Ellen knew exactly what Jack meant, as she often talked like that to her grandpa, remembering his stories about his home in Yorkshire and England's beautiful old buildings. Its cathedrals and bridges all built by hand and they'd lasted for centuries.

"We have something in common, Jack. We understand each other."

Ellen knew what kind of man she'd like to marry. Someone adventurous like her grandpa, who wasn't afraid to go places and try new things. A wise man who could talk about what mattered and what made you sad or confused. A man who says, 'I love you,' and means by that, 'I will cherish you and protect you.'

Ellen was beginning to believe she had met such a man.

Mary, Ellen, Frederick and William became a foursome, meeting at Ben and Elizabeth's hotel or with other youngsters in the area. Frederick had been in love with Mary since the day she had approached him at the funeral of his two sisters and brother-in-law.

The four visited family all around the peninsula: the Breitmeyers in German Bay, Frederick's home at the farm in Robinson's Bay, the Browns, the Pawsons and the Stevensons. They swam in the bays although Ellen was wary of the water. Her uncle had drowned in the harbour at German Bay when he was young, making her family cautious of the water ever since.

Frederick spent as much time with his uncle as he could, helping with the horses and joining in when the cocksfoot seed was ready for harvest. On one occasion he visited his aunt and uncle to find Ben was away on business in Addington. Elizabeth was clearing up the rubbish around the house and property and Frederick stayed to help. On that Wednesday a northerly wind was blowing and Elizabeth set the rubbish afire well away from the hotel and woolshed.

By one o'clock when Frederick and Elizabeth went in for lunch, the fire had nearly burnt itself out. Shortly after, a servant who had gone out for water ran back in, yelling, "Fire! Fire!"

Outside flames licked up and over the woolshed and stables. The alarm was given and seven men in the vicinity were soon on the scene to help Frederick. Unfortunately, the heat was so intense no one dared to approach the building, which burned down in front of their eyes. The shed was destroyed along with saddlery, harnesses, threshing clothes and tools for the cocksfoot seed harvest.

Ben arrived home to find the woolshed gone and his neighbour working to extinguish the last embers so that the valuable cocksfoot crops in the nearby paddocks would not go up in flames. Once they were all satisfied it was safe, the tired men trooped into the kitchen for a drink and a bite to eat.

Out of the blue, there was a blaze of fire between the kitchen and the dining room. The men formed a line from the creek to the house, but the fire had taken a hold beneath the house and there was no hope of saving it from destruction. Ben rescued his business accounts and some clothes; all the rest was lost.

Ben was devastated. After the helpers had returned to their homes, he went down to the creek to wash the soot from his body and the agony of loss from his heart. He pulled off his shirt, knelt beside the creek and began to splash his face and arms.

He didn't notice his nephew had followed him down. Frederick stared, unable to take his eyes off his uncle's back, criss-crossed with raised and ugly scars.

Ben realised what he had done.

"Lad, no-one but my brothers know of these scars; it's a secret that must be kept. I am the law here and what man would take notice if they knew the truth?"

"What happened to you, uncle?"

"Call it a matter of honour. Your Uncle George and I did some hard labour in a convict colony on Norfolk Island. We worked in the crank mill and sometimes in the sea, hacking coral from the reef to make lime for plaster and mortar. It was hard work and men sometimes swam away and out to sea to drown and end their misery."

"Men were angry and blamed each other so fights broke out over silly things. You had to hold your own, if you understand. On one occasion your uncle and I were pushed too far, a fight began and I was sentenced to the lash."

"So no-one has seen your back since you came to New Zealand? That's why you don't swim."

"You're right, I don't swim, but that's because I'm afraid of the water. Like many who were brought up away from the coast, I never learned to swim as a boy. I watched too many drown on the island. Now do I have your word? No one must know of my past."

Of all the Shadbolt men sent to Norfolk Island, Ben was to achieve the greatest changes in his circumstances. A man who took great pleasure in his possessions, loving his home, his land and his prize animals. The deprivations he had suffered were a powerful driving force, along with two strong partners who understood his potential.

Firstly Carolyn, whom he believed he had let down. Then Elizabeth, who comprehended the passion that led him to fake their past and live in luxury and good standing.

Now Frederick knew his secret, Ben began to share his story with his nephew.

"We owe the family left behind, struggling to make what they could of their lives in Datchworth, to do the best we can with ours. Eleanor took the young women under her wing, holding the family together. After your great-uncle Solomon died, she remarried and moved to Penge."

"Your Uncle George's wife Harriet followed Eleanor after their little girl Georgina died. Georgina was only four years of age, a sweet child named after her father, your uncle. She had brought great joy to the women, who suffered her loss greatly. These women battled together to make a life for themselves despite all the grief and pain they had endured."

"Jemima moved to Carshalton nearby and became

proprietor of the Railway Tavern, where she stayed until she was ninety-eight years old, outliving her daughter Martha by many years."

Ben continued to share with Frederick how he had learned to survive the years of degradation on Norfolk Island.

"We had to live in a world of dreams and illusions, believing that at the end of our sentence we would somehow lead the kind of life we all desire. A life with a wife who loves and supports you, and children a father can care for, and spoil a little. To be able to indulge in interests that fill a man with enthusiasm, and put enough food on the table to feed his family, and share with visitors."

Frederick knew there was more to the story than could be told in full because there was more pressing work to be done. He obliged his uncle with the promise to keep his secret, but nothing would be the same again.

Knowing their story changed how he felt about his uncle and his father. His was a family living with so many secrets and untruths. He wanted no more deceit or half-truths that could surface at any time to haunt his family.

Frederick declared his love for Mary and they married in 1876. The young couple moved away from Banks Peninsula to live in Oxford. Here they bought land and began a family that was to number eleven by the turn of the century.

Jack Wallace and Ellen married in 1878, one year after her mother Katerina died in childbirth. They stayed in Akaroa where Jack had built a successful business as a blacksmith, maintaining the wagons for Cobb and Co stage coaches.

Chapter 19

More than forty years have passed since the Breitmeyers and the Pawsons arrived in New Zealand; and twenty years since John Pawson and his friend Peter Brown were murdered in the goldfields.

Most of the forest has been cut down or burnt. The cocksfoot seed, which was difficult to harvest and required much labour, became uneconomical and has been taken over by other grasses. Work has become short and the next generation is expanding.

Ellen and Jack Wallace and Mary and Frederick Shadbolt needed employment to raise their families and build a nest egg for their old age. They had heard stories of the Pohangina Valley in the Manawatu, a rich valley of bush, some of which had been cleared to make way for agriculture. The Pohangina River supplied water as it flowed from the magnificent Ruahine Ranges southwards to meet the Manawatu River nearby.

Mary and Frederick Shadbolt were the first to make the courageous move to the North Island, settling in Pohangina. It is difficult to imagine how arduous it was in the 1880s to move with four children from the South Island to the North Island, but obviously the pioneering instinct remained in this family.

There was no regular shipping service across Cook Strait; that wouldn't happen for another ten years. In the early 1880s it was a case of waiting for the next ship passing through the port of Lyttelton. Cook Strait has a reputation as one of the most dangerous in the world, especially the voyage from Lyttelton up the coast to Wellington. In a rough crossing, coats hanging on wall hooks would end up flying out parallel to the floor, like ghosts come to haunt. The passengers were pleased to leave the heaving motion of the ship to disembark in Wellington.

The Shadbolts booked passage on a Cobb & Co coach for the trip north, which began well enough on developed roads close to the city. Further afield, roads turned into bullock tracks or very often the tracks Maori had walked and run over for years. The horses and coach drivers, or whips as they were referred to, had to negotiate as best they could. Sometimes passengers were asked to disembark while the horses pulled the coach through muddy potholes. Mothers held the children's hands tightly while fathers, in formal Victorian attire, helped to push the coach.

Later the family moved to Mangatainoka near Pahiatua in the Wairarapa valley. This journey, although shorter, was scary, if exciting. They had to travel through the Manawatu Gorge formed by the Manawatu River as it cut through the Ruahine Ranges.

The road on the southern side of the river had no fences or barriers between the road and the long drop into the river. Except for passing bays at intervals, there was only room for one coach at a time.

Ultimately the trip proved worthwhile because land was being sold cheaply and work was plentiful. The family flourished, and sent word to encourage Ellen and Jack to join them.

Before long Jack and Ellen Wallace, along with Ellen's father William Pawson and his second wife Juliet, decided they too would make the trip across the Strait. They purchased land on offer, sight unseen, in Eketahuna, south of Mangatainoka in the Wairarapa.

The sea voyage was expensive with little offered as refreshment for the travellers. The families consoled themselves with the knowledge that the best seamen had been employed to bring them safely to Wellington, a go-ahead and productive city that all agreed would prosper.

Wellington had become the capital city of New

Zealand in 1865, and boasted a safe harbour that was central to the entire country. William saw amazing growth since he had lived in the developing town all those years ago.

This added a sense of relief, given the risky move they were making to a place none of them had visited before.

The family boarded the morning train for Eketahuna, enjoying the panoramic views as it wound its way around the harbour towards Petone. The journey continued into the Hutt Valley, firstly Lower Hutt where the houses were set in gardens spacious enough for children to play in. Upper Hutt was less populated and formed the gateway to the Rimutaka Ranges.

The hills were covered in dark green bush that stretched far out on every side of the carriages as the train travelled along the top ridge. The track went through tunnels where black smoke seeped into the carriage. Most disturbing were the open spaces where high winds rocked the carriages. Wind-breaks had been built in some parts so that heavy gust would not derail the train.

At the summit, another engine was fitted to the train to prepare it for the one in fifteen grade decline. Once the train was safely down from the mountain, the passengers could see how the land opened up into the Wairarapa Valley with its paddocks full of sheep. Then they got a first glimpse of Lake Wairarapa, named for its glistening waters.

The houses were large and well kept, though already the gorse brought to the country by the early settlers was spreading, indicating that the area had been settled for a considerable period of time. The gorse that had made good stock hedges in the British Isles, here became a noxious weed, a curse to farmers all over New Zealand.

The train chugged along through Featherston, Greytown and Masterton, reaching the end of the line at Eketahuna by early afternoon.

The family were not disappointed as they compared the country they had travelled through with the homes they had left behind. In their minds, Wellington harbour was equal to Lyttelton harbour and the grass grew as well in the pastures here as it did in Akaroa. The beauty of the Rimutaka Range was comparable to the hills in Akaroa.

The good news spread and other family members migrated, some to the Pohangina Valley, some to Feilding, others to Pongaroa but all around the same area in the North Island. John Pawson planned to bring his sawmill to Feilding.

William Pawson bought 240 acres of land fronting onto Alfredton Road in Pleckville, just out of

Eketahuna, and settled into some farming. He became the postmaster, a position he kept until his death in 1903, sixty-three years after leaving his home town of Otley.

There was plenty of work for all the men, in the timber milling industry or as blacksmiths and wheelwrights. The land gave them extra income and allowed them to grow their own food, and stock for meat and milk.

A land that was now their own.

Part 3:
Turn of the Century

Chapter 20

Hannah Shadbolt, who had just turned seventeen, was about to travel by coach from Mangatainoka through the Manawatu Gorge to Palmerston North.

Hannah liked to buy the cotton for her fancy work from a little store that stocked many colours to choose from. She also took time to look for a little something to put into her glory box – a pretty nightgown or petticoat, perhaps. Like most young girls, Hannah sewed and crocheted 'things for her box': tablecloths, napkins, tea towels, pillowcases and doilies. All packed away ready for the day she married.

Palmerston North was a city well laid out with shops surrounding a square of grass where shoppers could tie their horses to hitching posts. It was an easy city for Hannah to get around, and she could call into as many shops as she wanted while visiting.

Hannah stepped onto the first step of the coach, but the second step, like all stairs, was awkward and painful for her, so she quickly shifted her weight to the next step. Hannah's left leg was withered as a result of infant polio, which had contracted the muscles, making it shorter than the right leg. The ankle was turned inwards, so that the weight was on the outside of her foot and ankle. The weight of her body would cause sores to form that became ulcerated and difficult to heal.

A gentleman boarded after her and spoke politely to Hannah.

"I prefer to sit that side to face the direction we're travelling. Do you mind if I take that empty seat next to you?"

Hannah patted the seat in affirmation, pleased to have company. Conversation flowed easily between them, especially when the coach travelled through the Manawatu Gorge, a favourite part of the trip for Hannah. The road still ran through the narrow gorge with no barrier between the road and the drop to the rapids below. The hills that rose sharply from the river were covered in bush and at one point a waterfall tumbled down behind the railway. It was a spectacular and dangerous road in those days. When the railway was built in 1891 this became the only river, road and rail gorge in the southern hemisphere.

"My mother remembers her first ride through this gorge," Hannah reminisced. "I was only a toddler then.

She often talks about how we moved to Mangatainoka, but I think she found travelling the gorge a bit scary. My parents, three of my siblings and I came to the Manawatu River by coach from Pohangina, where we had to climb into a canoe to get to the other side of the river to board a second coach."

"Yes," her fellow-traveller agreed, "it would have been very scary back then. The whips were brave men, travelling on unformed roads much of the time, fording rivers in many cases. Things have improved in the last few years. By the way, I'm Dr Dawson. May I know your name?"

Hannah had an urge to hide her ankle, not knowing exactly why because a doctor of all people would surely understand, but somehow she felt ashamed.

"Hannah," she replied. "Hannah Shadbolt."

Hannah was often asked to explain why her leg was as it was, and it had always been difficult for her. Polio, or infantile paralysis as it came to be known when it affected children, was uncommon in New Zealand in the 1800s. It was not until 1914 when the first epidemic occurred that people became more aware of its effects.

The treatment in the nineteenth century was untested and of little use, Hannah's parents would have struggled to get proper care for their little girl.

In the eighteenth century, the disease was believed to be a degeneration of the spinal cord. Not until advances in microscopy made possible the development of the 'germ theory,' was it established by the Viennese immunologist, Karl Landsteiner, that the disease was a viral infection.

"Hannah, I think our meeting today might have been fate, I'd like to speak with you when we reach our destination if that is all right with you."

Dr Dawson escorted Hannah to a tearoom where he ordered refreshments for himself and Hannah. He gently introduced the topic of her damaged leg, and she soon found herself telling him all about it.

What he proposed was a shock to Hannah, but she listened intently as Dr Dawson explained the benefits as best he could.

"Your lower leg is a burden to you. The continual ulceration of your ankle can only get worse as you get older and cause you more pain. When you get married, the extra weight of carrying a child will put even more strain on your spine. You deserve to stand straight and tall, Hannah, and you would be able to walk up steps much easier."

As he talked, a bubble of excitement rippled through Hannah, settling in her solar plexus, where her hands were clasped in a tight ball as though to quell feelings almost too much for her. Would her parents agree to such a thing?

She tried to imagine what it would be like with only one leg.

"Would I still be able to ride my pony?"

He smiled.

"Oh yes, of course, I would only need to take the leg a little below the knee, the part so badly affected by polio. You would have a prosthetic limb fitted, and because it is your left leg you would put that in the stirrup and, with help, be seated in the saddle."

Hannah had suffered taunts at school because she could not run as fast as the other children, or climb trees with them. She had chosen to ignore the bullies and make the most of what she could do. Needlework was a favourite activity, stitching crinoline ladies in bonnets on tablecloths or embroidering the borders with rows of Forget-Me-Nots.

She also liked caring for her younger brothers and sisters. Hannah had nine siblings, one a baby born only this year. Best of all, was when she rode her pony, because she had the freedom to run and jump on an equal footing with her friends.

Dr Dawson met with Hannah's parents, Frederick and Mary Shadbolt. There was much to discuss, but the family felt safe in the hands of this man. Dr Dawson summed up the meeting by impressing on the family that the spirit and determination Hannah had shown to overcome her affliction were vital to the success of the amputation.

"Another important factor is that the knee joint is in good condition because you have kept yourself mobile, Hannah. Even though it has been difficult for you to walk properly, the circulation to the leg is excellent, I can see few risks to you and many benefits."

All agreed it was best for Hannah that the operation be performed. Times had changed from the days when such surgery was performed with nothing more than alcohol to numb the pain. The use of chloroform had become commonplace since Queen Victoria had consented to its use for the birth of her eighth child, Leopold. The pain-relieving liquid was described as soothing beyond measure.

Though hygiene in many hospitals remained haphazard, all surgical instruments were sterilised because some heed was given to the germ theory.

The operation was successful and healing went well with no infection, though it took many weeks for the wounds to heal enough for Hannah to be fitted with her artificial leg. Made of iron and wood, the prosthesis was heavy to manipulate.

While the leg was healing, Hannah would kneel the left stump on a chair then hold the back of the chair and walk it forward a step, following up with a normal step with her right leg, then walking the chair forward again.

This was a technique Hannah used for the rest of her life. She moved around using her chair until she was ready to strap her on leg for the day.

There was more to learning how to master the prosthesis than Hannah had imagined. First she must learn to walk again, then practise bending down to pick things up. Discovering how to sit down on a chair was awkward to begin with, as was standing up again without losing her balance. She was compensated for her hard work by the excitement of being able to wear boots or pretty shoes on both feet.

The family knew that if they had not moved from the South Island, Hannah would never have met Dr Dawson, the man who changed her life. Now she was like any other young woman, could walk normally and was able to get work looking after children for a local family.

Hannah began to attend social events that she had usually avoided and it wasn't long before she attracted the attention of a handsome young man, by the name of Richard Wallace. He had moved with his parents Jack and Ellen Wallace to the Wairarapa from Akaroa when he was seven years old. Richard's father was a cavalry man during the New Zealand Land Wars in Taranaki. The family owned horses and Jack Wallace encouraged all his children to ride and become expert horsemen.

Richard visited Hannah's home and began to assist with her riding. He attended show jumping events in the district as her assistant. He presented her with a new side saddle and mounting block so that she could mount the pony without help.

"The mounting block will avoid the saddle slipping to the left side when you mount," he explained. "Then you can bend your right leg across in front of you, so it is between the pommels on either side of the seat. Safe as a church you'll be."

This method gives the rider an emergency grip by pressing the right calf against the saddle and the left thigh into the leaping head of the saddle. The rider is locked into this position, gaining extra support if the horse decides to buck or the rider has to make an unexpected jump.

Richard was making sure Hannah was as safe as possible so that she didn't injure herself. His tuition along with Hannah's natural talent meant she did well in events, and that gave her a sport where she could compete on equal terms against able-bodied contenders.

Hannah's involvement in community work included teaching Sunday school in the local Anglican Church. Richard knew this would not sit well with his father.

Jack understood what problems could arise from a mixed marriage. He had not forgotten the priest who had managed to force a separation between his parents, Arthur and Mary Wallace.

Jack believed that it had ultimately led to the death of his brother Richard, who had joined the army to get away from a stepfather he had no time for.

This presented a problem that seemed insurmountable to the young man who had fallen in love with Hannah. He knew it would be hard to find a woman with such determination and courage. Hannah was the woman he wanted to share his life with.

Hannah herself suggested a solution

"There is only one way to deal with your father's fears, Richard. We will both renounce our faith. I will burn my prayer book and you can do the same with your rosary beads. We will not allow religion to rule our lives any further, or the lives of those we love."

Richard believed this would bring an end to his father's fears. He was wrong. He told his parents of the plan, then sat out the awkward silence that followed. His father filled his pipe with tobacco, pressed it down firmly and reached for a match to light it. Finally, he spoke the words that would echo in Richard's mind for the rest of his life.

"Can't you find yourself a girl that has two good legs?"

There was no quelling the bitterness held on to by Jack, who was now using Hannah's disability as an excuse to split up the pair. He would prefer them to separate than face the complications of a mixed marriage.

The young couple did not listen. Instead, they built a fire and solemnly threw the symbols of their religion into the flames. Such was the love that had flourished between the two, who married in Eketahuna in 1905.

Richard and Hannah set up home in Pahiatua and Richard became a volunteer fireman. He also drove the stage coach that delivered mail as far as Pongaroa.

The rural mail delivery was of considerable importance in those days, all communications being delivered by post, whether job applications, birthday and Christmas cards, wedding invitations or birth announcements. The old adage, 'The mail must get through,' was faithfully adhered to, though it wasn't always easy. Narrow, winding roads, prone to mud slips, made journeys dangerous in many places.

Richard's younger brother John worked for him on the mail coach until he was killed in a freak accident. John picked up mail at the Rakanui store, which doubled as the post office. The road was muddy that day, and as the mail coach rounded a bend, the road fell away in front of it. The coach overturned, trapping John underneath and he suffocated in the soft mud. One of the horses broke free and returned to the store, alerting the owners something was amiss. They rode out and discovered the tragic truth.

On one occasion a bush fire stopped the mail coach from getting through. The wind was blowing a gale, spreading the blaze towards the local mill. A stack of timber caught fire and soon surrounding houses and stables were totally destroyed.

The local doctor, one of the first to own a car, was motoring to attend the son of the Rakanui store who had been injured. A burning branch fell onto the car and hit the doctor on his head, causing a fatal wound. Another life lost to the dangers that beset the early settlers. Inadequate roads, the threat from fires, the many risks of the forestry industry and drowning were to take many good people.

It wasn't long before Richard discovered a little adjunct to his mail delivery, supplying a market for whisky and rum to farmers, bushmen and shearers. He loaded his mail coach with a few barrels and pocketed the cash.

Life was good and our nation was growing up. The year of Richard and Hannah's wedding day happened to coincide with the first time the All Blacks rugby team toured internationally. They played against the British Isles, France and the USA during 1905-1906. The Wallaces became avid supporters of what was to become New Zealand's national sport.

The All Blacks took the world by storm, winning an opening game against Devon in England by 55-4. Some papers printed the score the wrong way round because it was such an unexpected win. The team defeated every English side they faced and it wasn't until they met Wales at Cardiff Arms Park that they suffered a 3-nil defeat. But not without controversy, questions being raised over an All Black try being disallowed that would have brought them level.

The team went on to produce some of the most popular sports athletes in the world. Since their debut against Australia in 1903 the All Blacks have won three Rugby World Cups 1987 and back to back in 2011 and 2015. They have a seventy-six percent winning record in test matches and since the introduction of world rugby rankings in 2003 New Zealand has been ranked first longer than all the other teams combined.

In 2016 they won a record eighteen consecutive test matches without a loss, statistics confirming them as the best team ever in rugby history.

Chapter 21

1914 was an election year and the beginning of World War One. The good times that had allowed New Zealand to develop its overseas exports were over, and a time of austerity was to begin for New Zealand.

The country was dependent on Mother England as a market for wool, frozen meat and dairy products, the dominant industries that kept New Zealand's economy afloat.

As early as 1909, the Prime Minister had responded to a perceived German threat by announcing that New Zealand would fund the building of a battlecruiser for the Royal Navy. The cost of £1.7 million pounds would equate to a $300,000,000 investment one hundred years on.

HMS New Zealand joined the first Battlecruiser Squadron of the Grand Fleet in the Baltic Sea. It was to take on a distinct New Zealand flavour when Captain Green wore a Maori piupiu, a skirt made from flax, and a greenstone tiki pendant during battles, items presented to him in 1913 during a tour of New Zealand.

The ship saw action in the battles of Heligoland Bight, Dogger Bank and Jutland, suffering minimal damage and few casualties. She became known as the lucky ship, her good fortune attributed to the wearing of the piupiu and tiki.

By the time the war broke out Richard and Hannah had five children. The family had been doing well in Pahiatua where Richard's sideline liquor business was thriving. Richard was unable to enlist after suffering an injury when he slipped down a ladder at a fire he was attending. The injury, his age and the size of his family meant he would not be sent overseas.

His brother, George, fought and was killed in the Battle of the Somme in 1918. His youngest brother, Alex, played an essential role, stationed at VLB Awarua Radio. This Post and Telegraph Telecommunications Station was situated between Invercargill and Bluff in the South Island. The station was notable because of its effective transmissions over great distances, which turned out to be of great value during the war years.

The Post and Telegraph offices were the enlistment centres for soldiers, with men who were called up notified by telegram. The army barracks were based in Featherston, which meant that particular post office became one of the busiest in the country. The post office savings bank was the bank used by most workers so many of the soldiers had their pay deposited into that account allowing the bank to flourish.

Schools played an active role in the war effort, putting on dances and concerts to raise money. Items performed often pertained to military themes. One innovative idea was to build a copper trail, laying penny and halfpenny coins from Auckland to Wellington. School children the length of the North Island eagerly added their coins to the trail.

Hannah and the Wallace children knitted socks and scarves and wrote letters that were posted to the front line. In many cases the letters were answered by lonely soldiers, creating a close connection between sender and recipient. Children were encouraged to stay cheerful and help their parents so that families with sons or husbands fighting overseas would be less stressed.

More than one thousand teachers enlisted in the army leaving a shortfall in the schools, many of which were one teacher schools. Lesson plans were published to help inexperienced tutors and parents who filled in during the war. *The School Journal* was full of articles on key battles, with maps included.

Children learned to march and obey orders, a

discipline continued in secondary schools into the 1950s. They were expected to help with domestic chores as more women were engaged to assist the non-fighting men in the workforce. Generally, there was a call for discipline and patriotism which, as time would tell, proved to be a forerunner to World War II. This was a conflict in which these young children would become the main players.

The strong prohibition movement in New Zealand since the late 1800s had lapsed, but the urgent need for more efficiency in the workforce brought the matter to the forefront again. During 1915 and 1916, 160,000 people signed a petition for pubs to close at six o'clock. The Government agreed to this temporary wartime measure in 1917, maybe in the hopes that the lobby for prohibition would lose traction. By 1919 the prohibition movement was defeated, by a very narrow margin.

Six o'clock closing brought about what became known as 'the six o'clock swill'. This was a time when men rushed to the pubs after work and ordered their beer from a keg, buying enough to last beyond six o'clock when the cash register would be closed.

The law was to remain in place until 1967 when patrons ordered beer by the jug. The bartender lined up the jugs and walked along filling them with a dispenser. New Zealand was allowed to grow up, and for the first time food was served with the drink, bar meals at first but later fully licensed restaurants.

Richard did not see six o'clock closing as a good thing because he enjoyed his drink and the social contact it provided. Hannah, on the other hand, was pleased to have him home with their ever-expanding family. By 1924 the couple had ten children, six sons and four daughters.

During the WW1 the Pahiatua area was kept busy and buoyant with the milling of trees. Wood was an important commodity during a war fought from trenches lined with timber. This was a war where mud clogged soldiers' boots, requiring wooden paths to be built around headquarters in the combat zones.

Richard's father Jack was still employed in the industry and he encouraged Richard to become a part of it to ensure a secure future. In 1919 Hannah and the family moved to Kahiku, near Pongaroa, to work in Yeoman's timber mill but by 1921 the tide changed and the boom ended. Times became more difficult. Richard did whatever he could to bring in extra money. He looked after the big horses that were used at the mill and the oxen that pulled the logs out of the forest.

Life in the small country mill town was all the younger children knew. They walked without shoes to school each day along the verges of a gravel road, pleased when the grader had been because the shoulder was smooth with dirt rather than gravel digging into their feet. All their toys were homemade: marbles made of clay, skipping ropes from ends left lying around at the mill. An old mill horse named Wallace pulled them around on a homemade sledge as they gathered firewood from under the pine trees.

There were limestone caves to explore in the hills behind the house. The youngest was sent into the smaller passages with a candle and a reel of cotton so that he could find his way out again. The creeks were full of fresh-water crayfish that the children gathered for their meals on the weekends, delicious with a slice of bread and dripping. Equivalent to takeaways in today's towns, when you lived in the country and Mum needed a break from cooking.

Richard enjoyed the extra work of looking after the mill animals, but it was also what led to the worst possible scenario for the family. Richard had occasion to kill and skin an oxen that had been injured. It turned out the oxen had TB, which Richard contracted and by 1927 at the age of forty-eight he was dead. Hannah was left with her ten children just as the Great Depression set in, with no widow's benefit to lessen the blow.

The marriage the couple had worked so hard to make a success was to end not because of differing religious beliefs, the fears of an earlier generation, but because of an unexpected and debilitating disease.

Hannah contacted the Catholic priest to bury her husband and the Anglican minister to baptise her children. All ten children, almost completely ignorant of religious ceremonies, were told to kneel in the front room of their home as the minister sprinkled each of them with holy water. The pact was broken and Hannah could attend church once more.

Pongaroa held nothing for the family now so Hannah moved to Dannevirke where her children could get work and help out financially. Three of the older daughters were sent out to work, and encouraged to find husbands. This they did, and all three wed within two years of their father's passing.

Hannah now had seven children to feed. Two sons were older than fourteen so were able to work. The other five were aged from eleven years to three years old. Hannah worked scrubbing and cleaning houses, and grew vegetables in the garden, served with bread, spread with bacon fat when she could afford it.

The burden was too great. Hannah had no choice but to allow three of her youngest sons to be sent to a Salvation Army home to be cared for. The shame and grief was almost more than she could bear, with her beloved children living too far away for her to visit. She could see things were not going to get better, only worse, because work was desperately short for everyone.

The years that followed were most grim in New Zealand's history. Wool and meat markets plummeted, with exports dropping by forty-five percent in two years. Farmers were making no money and their efforts to increase production of butter and cheese only made the situation worse, ending in a negative income by 1932. The country was not prepared for this level of unemployment and there was no provision for relief as there was in Britain, and even Australia.

In 1935 a Labour Government brought in a welcome cradle to the grave care system, an end at last to the eight years Hannah had struggled with the small income she and her two sons could earn. The boys had found work scrub-cutting and working on farms with plough horses.

Both jobs paid poorly and the living conditions provided were appalling. Huts that looked like they had been built by school boys to play in, some nothing more than a lean-to built beside a dirt bank with a corrugated iron roof sloping away to take the water into a gutter dug in the earth. The windows and doors were covered with nothing but sacking to keep out the wind and rain.

A corrugated iron shed with windows and a proper

door was a luxury even with its dirt floor. These huts had a lantern and a one-element kerosene cooker so you could make porridge in the mornings and stew in the evening.

All the family's clothes were patched, with shoes passed down, often too small. Sheets were cut in half when they became thin, and the two sides turned and sewn together in the middle. The government pension improved the family's diet considerably. Fruit delivered from Hawkes Bay was bottled for the winter. Meals of tripe and onions with white sauce were now possible, along with cheaper cuts of meat for stews and casseroles.

At last the younger children could come home. They were thin, reserved and shy of their mother and siblings, with no sparkle in their eyes. They ate every scrap of food put in front of them, scraping their plates clean with a knife or spoon.

In the darkest of days of the Depression the only daughter still at home missed her monthly period. Thirteen years of age and unsure why that had happened, she made what turned out to be a big mistake and mentioned it to her mother.

"You've shamed us and yourself, child. We have scrimped and scraped and you think you can sleep around and bring a baby into the world, another mouth to feed!"

"I have done nothing wrong! Why don't you believe me?"

Ignorance and fear prevailed and the young girl was quickly married to a man who was happy to acquire such a young and pretty bride. A deplorable sacrifice to the hard times that forced decisions based on poverty rather than truth.

As each of the children reached the age of fourteen they were sent off to work and for the first time there was enough money to afford small comforts. One of the boys was only thirteen years of age when he got a job driving, but he went willingly to support his mother.

Hannah's six boys grew into fine young men, the youngest only fifteen years old when once again there were rumours of war. The marching drills at school and the talk of glory for defending your country was ingrained in the psyche of these men.

Even though they were experiencing the joy of youth and the company of sweethearts, they could not resist the urge to walk into the post office and enrol.

Before long four of Hannah's six sons were wearing army uniforms. The oldest had been injured so was not eligible and the youngest was still under age. The second eldest had already been in training, but was recovering in the army hospital from surgery on hammer toes.

The brothers trained in different camps including Waiouru, Napier, and Solway in Masterton. The regular pay packet built up during this time and the boys saw an opportunity to take care of Hannah while they were away at war. They used their pooled earnings to buy her a house as a thank you for the years of struggle and the care she had given them, the hardships borne without complaint.

Hannah walked up the long drive and turned left at the path between the veranda and the rose bushes then up the steps into a cottage she could call her own.

The front door opened into a long hall, with a floral carpet runner down the centre with coloured stripes along the edges, and a polished timber floor on each side. Her aspidistra in a copper pot had been placed in the corner on the right, her umbrella stand a little further down, chenille curtains hanging half way down the hall were tied back against the wall.

The first two doors off the hall led into bedrooms, with two more bedrooms beyond the curtains.

At the end of the hall the door to the left opened into a scullery that would soon hold preserving jars of peaches, apricots, tomatoes and beans. The washroom was at the very end along with the copper for boiling the laundry.

The door on the right led into the dining room, which soon became the most used room in the home, large enough for a table that could seat twelve, as well as a couch on either side. Two chairs flanked the coal range at the far end. On the hearth was a bucket filled with coal and a shovel balanced on top ready to stoke the fire that heated a kettle for cups of tea.

Hannah never believed she would own a house of her own.

The family sat around the table for the first time, before long they were reminiscing about their childhood.

"Do you remember the marbles, Mum?" asked Chas.

This began a raucous outburst.

"Mine were blue."

"Mine were red."

"I wanted the red ones, but mine were green."

Hannah had made marbles out of clay and dyed them so that her children would know which were which. One day the children were called to lunch in the middle of a game and the ducks ate the marbles. For days a ritual poo inspection took place. A worthwhile endeavour because all the marbles were recovered except by now the dye had faded and all were a muddy grey.

Hannah had given her family a childhood to remember. Now they wanted her to have this home.

"It is yours. You can grow the garden you've always wanted, paint the kitchen the colours you want. You can do anything you please."

The quarter acre section developed over the years into a picture-book garden, with roses growing over trellised arches and beds of old English flowers, including gypsophila, trailing over the path. The front porch was where family photos were taken, with the family standing and smiling for the camera when they came to visit Hannah.

Chapter 22

1942, and once again three brothers named Wallace were heading to war, this time away from New Zealand and back to Europe to protect the lands of their ancestors.

Chas had been born on 11th of November, the date the armistice agreement was signed between Germany and the Allied powers. At 11am on that day in 1918, the guns fell silent. Time enough for a baby to grow up and volunteer for the war that followed the war to end all wars.

Wally was born during leap year on 29th of February 1920. Officially he had not celebrated four actual birthdays, yet was facing dangers he could not imagine. Ron, the youngest, always followed his best buddies and scraped in to join his brothers at eighteen years of age.

The three met in a camp in the Pauatahanui Valley near Wellington to make ready to board the ship

Aquitania. All ship movements were secret. No newspaper reports were to be written and the names of the ships were covered up, although *Aquitania*, a Cunard White Star liner, was easily recognised by her shape.

Hannah received word there would be no home leave for the 8th Reinforcement before the ships sailed overseas. She had a bad feeling about her boys leaving on the *Aquitania* so she feigned ill health. What army would send three brothers away without final leave from a widowed mother with one leg, who was unwell?

While the boys were visiting their mother on compassionate leave there had been a walk-out at the camp. The troops took it into their own hands to make a final visit home and the Wallace boys arrived back at Paekakariki train station to find a couple of hundred troops who'd been 'absent without leave' milling around as they wondered how to get back into camp without repercussions.

Ron had earned his sergeant's stripes and therefore he was the one to call them all into line. He put his brothers in the leading rank, and began to march the soldiers left, right, left along the road that led to the camp. The guard snapped to attention as Ron marched them through the gate until they were out of sight behind the tents. Then he gave the order, "fall out!"

Two hundred troopers disappeared more quickly than your ten-bob placed on a sure bet with a crooked bookie.

The Wallaces boarded the ship with eight thousand other soldiers from all over New Zealand. They had to wait for high tide before the *Aquitania* had enough water under her to sail. Amidst a wash of mud and sludge, she left port and headed south. Although it was December, the troops wore greatcoats and balaclavas against the cold blowing straight off floating icebergs.

Ron had ditched his stripes and joined his brother Wally in the service company, trucking ammunition, water, and sometimes wounded men. This meant they met up with each other on duty, and on occasions saw Chas. With such meetings they kept each other's spirits up when things got bad.

All three played a role in the battle at Cassino in the early part of 1944. This difficult assault was to be the most brutal and costly involving New Zealand forces in the World War II. A controversial decision was made to bomb the monastery that overlooked the town of Cassino. The bombing did little to minimise Allied casualties and most of the Germans survived the attacks.

Many of the bombs landed at some distance from

the monastery, and the craters left behind filled with water after the Germans knocked down stop banks on the Rapido River. A botched aerial attack came two days too early before the New Zealand Infantry was ready to advance, but Lieutenant-General Sir Bernard Freyberg proceeded with the attack anyway.

The New Zealanders were to attack Cassino from the south while the Indian Division came in from the North; the objective being to open a passage for the allies into the Liri Valley.

The soldiers had to make their way through the craters and across the swollen river. The 28th Maori Battalion initiated an attack on the well-defended railway station. All New Zealanders fighting together on a front that would eventually fall allowing allied entry into Rome on 4th of June.

This was two days before the D-Day landings in Normandy, making the Italian initiative a secondary theatre of operations. The New Zealand role became one of tying down German forces that could otherwise have moved to defend its position in France and Germany itself.

By this time the youngest brother, Dick, had lied about his age and got himself into the middle of things, firstly in the Pacific where he was supposed to guard Japanese prisoners of war who were to be exchanged for New Zealand prisoners. Before they reached the island where the prisoners were held, the Americans had begun an invasion and the ship with Dick Wallace aboard was sunk.

He was picked up by a battleship; unbelievably, this too was hit. He spent four hours in the water before he was rescued and taken to an American field hospital, suffering from a tropical fever.

Young, fit and indestructible, the young soldier went into a nearby town with a couple of Americans who were also in recovery. He was returned to the hospital with a knife in his ribs. Finally, he was shipped back to New Zealand to recuperate. His second posting was to Egypt where his age was discovered and he was enrolled in an army cooking course.

By now his brothers knew Dick was in the war zone, but they had been unable to trace his company. Word came through the grapevine that the mobile cookhouse had been in an accident and gone off the road. After many enquiries, Dick was traced in a British casualty clearing station (CCS.)

The brothers tracked him down to discover he had been sitting on a bunk with his shoulder slumped and multiple bruising. He had been like this for a week with no attention; apparently the British only looked after their own. They bundled him into the water carrier they had taken without permission and took him to a New Zealand CCS. After his recovery, he was transferred to Hawaii.

Bill, the soldier who had surgery on his feet that exempted him from service, lived in fear that one of his four siblings would be killed. The letters he received telling of the close shaves they had all experienced did little to quell his fear. He had been jointly responsible for keeping them fed and sheltered when they were small, becoming a father figure for them after their father died. Now they were on their own.

Bill was twenty-eight years old and married with a son when the army lost a soldier to experimental surgery. The surgeons were of the opinion that they could improve the marching ability of men with hammer toes by removing the phalanges bones from the offending toes. The results were as bad as the idea itself.

The biomechanics of the ankle and feet work beautifully with the phalanges intact, and not at all well without them. The patient cannot toe-off properly, so walks with a shuffle and a limp.

Once Bill had been discharged from the army he purchased a rural mail contract. Mail and telegrams were the only means by which messages could be sent, letters from the soldiers, birthday greetings, bills, invitations, draft notices and the telegrams sent when a son or husband or brother was killed.

Bill also delivered grocery items to the farmers, who were not encouraged to enlist. The production of food was vital to feed the nation and, more importantly, the troops. On the home front, there was already rationing of sugar, butter, cheese, tea, and petrol and clothing coupons. Petrol and butter remained rationed until June 1950.

Six months after the war in the Pacific began American soldiers were sent to New Zealand either to rest after coming out of horrific battles or to prepare for their turn to fight. The American Invasion, as it was known, was the first culture shock since the early days of immigration.

These men spoke our language, yet made it sound unlike anything most New Zealanders had heard because of the accent and because many words had different meanings.

They had money and gifts to share and entertainments such as baseball and jazz concerts. They were the reason hamburgers, doughnuts and Coca Cola took a foothold in this country. The soldiers were welcomed and the economy came to no harm with the extra cash flow spent on taxis, dry-cleaning and extra food.

The single girls were fascinated by the outgoing, fun-loving Americans, but for some they brought heartache. Pregnancies were inevitable. Some ended well and the mothers followed their men and settled in America after the war. Others were left with a baby to raise on their own, bringing hardship and the stigma that accompanied such a decision.

On a few occasions, a soldier would take responsibility and the baby was taken back to America and adopted by his family. In this case the mother would suffer the pain of never seeing her child again. In extremely rare cases, when the child was old enough, it would seek out the mother, meetings fraught with problems though the desire on the part of the child was completely understandable.

New Zealand soldiers were also affected when some of them received Dear John letters from sweethearts. The young women were tired of waiting for the men to return and chose to live for the moment.

The Wallace brothers were relieved their girlfriends lived miles away from where the Americans were camped. In the meantime, they continued to fight bravely and keep their heads down in hopes of returning to those they loved. They did survive, though not without some near misses. On one occasion, Chas and Ron had met up on the top floor of a building for a yarn when a shell hit the wall they were leaning against. Both were hurled across the room and left concussed. This did give the boys a few days away from the front.

Like so many of the men who fought in World War II, their scars ran deep though the horror of war was never talked of, but kept locked inside. Life for Hannah's carefree boys would never be the same. Alcohol and cigarettes became the popular means of numbing the memories. Five years had passed of young men serving in a useless war that stole men's innocence and, for some, their sanity.

Twelve thousand New Zealand soldiers killed out of a population of two million.

Chapter 23

A small town in New Zealand, 1942

I was born in November 1942, during World War II, almost one year after Japan bombed Pearl Harbour in Hawaii.

The bombing was both a shock and a relief to New Zealanders because now the United States entered the war. German raiders and armed merchant ships had been active in New Zealand waters and when America began using New Zealand as a base for soldiers on leave, the citizens felt safer.

By the time I was born, the US Navy had won the Battle of the Coral Sea, turning the tide in favour of the Allies.

My father, Bill, had been medically discharged from the army but four of my uncles were overseas, fighting for the country our ancestors – Shadbolts, Wallaces, Pawsons and Breitmeyers – had made their home one hundred years ago.

My grandmother, Hannah Shadbolt, fell in love with and married her second cousin Richard Wallace, and the blood of all these early settlers runs deep in my veins.

My first childhood memory was just after the war before I turned three years of age. I was living with my grandmother Hannah because my mother was hospitalised for almost two years. I remember playing under the dining room table, the tablecloth hanging down to make a tent where I could take my toys and create my own little world.

My grandmother was an amputee, a handicap she managed well when she was raising her own ten children. Now her age made it difficult for her to bend down and pick me up, bathe me or tie my shoe laces.

I learned quickly how to look after myself, keeping out of her way as much as possible. I referred to Hannah as 'big Gran' not because she was fat, but tall and bosomy, and somewhat overpowering for a little girl. I don't remember seeing either of my two brothers while I lived with Gran or even my father, although I do recall someone hugging me who wore scratchy clothes. That might have been him.

The sharpest memory I have concerns my grandmother's wooden leg. Hannah began each day without her prosthesis, moving around to prepare breakfast by resting her stump on a chair, taking a step with the good leg then moving the chair forward and so on.

Even at three years old I was aware of two things when Gran was walking with her chair. Firstly, that it was a slow method of getting around; and, secondly, it was best to keep out of the way of the chair as it lumbered forward.

At about 10 o'clock in the morning Gran would make a cup of tea, and the leg would appear, wearing a thick brown stocking and a black shoe with narrow brown leather straps dangling down from the top. Before putting on her leg, Gran massaged her stump with petroleum jelly. The smell of this oil based emollient, wafting into my nostrils triggers those memories to this day.

The stump, which ended just below her knee, was now wrapped in gauze. Gran wrapped it firmly, using both hands to ensure it covered the end of the stump where there were scars and red patches. I can still see her patting the ends of the gauze flat on the inside of the leg. Next came a roll of red flannel, a fabric that gave some cushioning, but was prickly to touch. This was carefully wrapped over the gauze, keeping it as smooth as possible.

Gran now shuffled forward on the couch so that her leg straightened out, with the stump bent at the knee so that it was pointing slightly towards the floor.

Gran picked up the artificial leg. I could tell it was heavy but Gran was strong, she flicked the straps to the side and at last the stump disappeared into the hollow leg, the straps were buckled up and the job was done.

Because of the weight of the leg – and apparently it didn't fit too well – the stump was rubbed and became inflamed. At night she would dab it with methylated spirits on cotton wool to stop infection and to toughen the skin. But Gran never complained.

I went home to my mother and father when I was three and a half. My younger brother was there with us, but my older brother stayed with our other grandmother. My younger brother was eighteen months old, but had never been put on the ground and hadn't learned to walk. He was born with a cleft palate that had required twelve operations so far.

The operations were carried out in Basham, a private hospital established by Dr H. P. Pickerell, in Wellington. As it turned out New Zealand had two of the leading specialists in plastic and reconstructive surgery in Dr Pickerell and his wife Dr Cecily Pickerell. Up until the first and second World Wars this specialist surgery had remained in its infancy.

The horrific injuries that had occurred during both wars had contributed to a greater knowledge of facial reconstruction.

My brother was lucky to have Dr Cecily Pickerell, with her excellent reputation, operate on his face and palate. She was delighted, saying his skin was the best she had ever worked on, making her work easier and producing results she was proud of.

The district nurse who cared for my brother between the many operations was afraid he would get an infection and was unwilling to allow him on the floor.

My next most vivid memory is of teaching my brother to walk. I would stand him up to get his balance, putting a pillow behind him in case he fell. Sure enough, he would plop down onto the pillow and we would try again. When he got the hang of standing and began to step forward, I would crawl behind him with the pillow at the ready.

My growing-up years were full of sunshine, green lawns, tricycles, tea sets and tea parties. When I got older – seven, perhaps – my favourite game was catching birds. I would lean Dad's garden sieve on a broad stick with string tied around it, and scatter bread underneath. When wax-eyes and yellow hammers came to eat the bread, all I had to do was hide in the garage and keep watch, then pull the string. The sieve would fall and catch the bird, which I put in an empty aviary.

When I had about fifteen birds I would open the

aviary door and watch until one brave bird flew out; then the others would follow. My mother was a bird-lover and a founding-member of the local RSPCA and I'm surprised she let me do that to the poor little birds, which although unharmed probably disliked being trapped in the cage. Perhaps that was her equivalent to letting the children of today play on their iPads to keep them busy while mothers completed their chores.

There were very few rules in our home. We were expected to use our common sense and behave in a manner that would not embarrass our parents, and we did. My brothers and I swam in the river at the end of our street. The river was a long way down a steep hill. We ran down so fast it was difficult to stay on our feet.

"Bet I'm first in," my brother would yell as he flew across the field and down a bank to the deep swimming hole.

"I don't care. You have chased the eels away for me."

We would dive off the bank and into water that was always warm. There was never any adult with us but we never got hurt, even though we put ourselves at risk. We speared eels that are very hard to kill and would instantly slither back down the bank and into the river again.

We climbed trees and collected pinecones on our way home for Little Gran's cooker. Oh, yes. My Mum's mother – where my older brother lived – was a petite woman, hence the name. She baked rice pudding and jam tarts in her wood-fire stove.

I liked school. I was lucky because the system suited me. I had always been a child who did as I was told, and I paid attention in class and did well. It was in the school environment that I was impacted by the war in a personal way. I had just turned eight and was in Standard Two, my teacher was Mr Mac, who wore strange shoes with a bulbous toe. From memory, he could walk quite well, but it was hard not to stare at those unusual shoes. I never learned what had happened to his feet, though schoolyard whispers claimed 'it had happened in the war.'

Did the funny shoes invoke pity, or was I just a kid fascinated by something out of the ordinary? I don't know, but I certainly caused an emotional reaction from my teacher. I believe he was aware of the pity I felt for him and it made him angry enough to retaliate.

Our writing period was before lunch and each day I would lift the lid of my desk to bring out my exercise book and begin to copy the paragraph Mr Mac had written on the board for us.

As we wrote Mr Mac walked up and down between the desks, starting on the far side of the room well away from my desk. He tapped the odd book on his rounds, making a suggestion, or perhaps moving a book into a more suitable position. He always approached my desk from behind and would pick up my forearm and slam it down on the desk and begin shouting about the slope of my writing.

Every second day he would drag me by the arm out to the front of the class and use the strap, which was thick enough to hurt such a small hand. I would return to my desk, red of face, but without a tear. I was embarrassed and pleased it was nearly lunch time so I could escape the threat.

What is interesting is that I never told my parents. Teachers were always right, so I must have deserved the strap and I was probably afraid of being told off for tittle-tattling. I'm sure there are many stories of men stressed and angry from the war who made bad choices about how they treated their pupils, families and work colleagues.

One more side effect of the war.

I studied with the brighter students at High School, though nothing I was learning seemed relevant to me. I was hopeless at French, the only second language taught, and that hasn't changed over the years. I enjoyed history, which wouldn't get me a job. Cooking and sewing classes were easy and fun and did serve me well when I became a mother.

During my second year at High School I took a job in Woolworths variety store for the Christmas holidays, and discovered I enjoyed getting a pay packet. I never went back to school. My parents, who believed it was a waste of time educating girls 'because they ended up getting married anyway,' made no protest at my decision to leave my education behind.

I was soon promoted at Woolworths to the sweets counter, where it was regarded as a privilege to work. I was also put in charge of the grocery section, where staff were on a higher pay scale. I learned many skills working for Woolworths and brought some of my own to the job. Most importantly, the need for common-sense and the ability to add up quickly in my head, which I did with ease as the customers picked the tins and packets off the counter and handed them to me. No trolleys in those days!

After about a year the novelty had worn off. I began checking ads in the paper for another position, and applied for a job for an assistant in a paint and wallpaper shop. I got the job and decided this was more like it. I learned the basics of interior design, and enjoyed helping customers choose wallpaper and paint. My boss was great with colours and my skills rapidly improved as I listened to him and some of the customers who were clever with decorating. It's called 'learning on the job.'

Although I did well enough at school in sport, I didn't have the confidence to be much of a team player. A good friend introduced me to badminton and this turned out to be a great sport for me, keeping me out of trouble throughout my teen years.

My brothers were keen motorcyclists and I met boys in the club they went to, spending the weekends doing road trials. We were given a map with a marked course that usually ended at a milk bar. The idea was to reach our destination within a predetermined time, a good way to see the countryside and experience that closeness with nature a motorcycle allows the rider.

Sometimes the boys would go to a scrambling course on a farm somewhere, with the girls cheering them on. The best part was a picnic lunch, bacon and egg pie followed by cake. Much time was spent by my brothers in the garage, fixing said bikes. My older brother even took one apart in our lounge to get it ready for repainting. Like I said, not many rules at our home.

He worked on the bike in the evenings as we listened to the music we had recorded from the radio. There was always music in our home: Bill Haley's Comets with *Rock around the Clock*, and Elvis, right up there with Buddy Holly.

Consumerism had not taken a hold during my

childhood. The most significant 'luxury' item my parents bought was a refrigerator. We had a radio, a record player and a tape recorder. Most families could afford to buy a home. Ours was a villa not on the posh side of town, but near the shops, and about half way between the two primary schools.

My parents' money was spent mainly on 'doing up' the house, which meant connecting it to power rather than the gas lighting from the gas works. A hot water tank replaced the gas copper that was used to heat the water for washing clothes and filling up the bath tub. We didn't take a bath every day when the hot water had to be heated in the copper, and when we did the bath was never more than a few inches deep. No lying back in hot water up to our necks. As children we were often stood in the copper to be given a good wash, and off we went.

My mother was what I would now call high maintenance, a glamorous lady who dressed well in expensive clothes and shoes. She always looked great in the post-war styles borrowed from the French, the New Look, with its nipped-in waists and fuller, longer skirts, so welcome after the restrictions of wartime, and worn with hat and gloves.

My father, though not a spender, was a handsome man and dapper in his white scarf and the Trilby hat he always wore even though he had a great head of hair. I think he got stuck in the war years, not because he had fought in the war, but because he hadn't. There was a certain residue of guilt for not fighting with his brothers, even though he'd been discharged through medical misadventure by the military hospital.

Though people did take holidays I never heard of anyone taking a flight to Fiji or Australia. I'm sure some did, but most went to 'the coast,' which was never far away from any town in New Zealand. My family didn't go on long holidays because my father owned several rural mail contracts and there were few days when the mail was not delivered.

We always went to the Boxing Day race meeting at Awapuni races in Palmerston North. Dad gave us ten shillings and for one shilling we could buy a one-tenth share of his own ten-shilling bet on the horse of our choice. I would choose horses with names that included letters like J or K or Z.

This excellent method of picking a winner led me to choose *Dark Song*, a rank outsider, in the last race, which Dad referred to 'one for the jockeys.' *Dark Song* won by a mile, very exciting, assuring money enough for the next meeting in a year's time.

☆

I had left home by the time my parents bought one of the first televisions to come into the country. The programmes were in black and white and they had to drive to Wellington to buy it. There was a waiting list and none available in the small towns. I didn't own a TV until the 1970s. I was too busy saving for lounge and dining furniture.

Clothes and shoes were expensive back then. There were restrictions on imported goods and most things were made in our own country, which was good for employment but tough on parents' pockets. There was no money spent on designer jeans.

Until the 1970s Levi was not in our vocabulary, although tartan and chequered trousers were worn with a jumper from the 1950s onwards.

Chapter 24

I was sixteen when in 1958 I met the man I would later marry. That was the same year the Russian *Luna 2* unmanned spacecraft landed on the moon.

TC was good at all sport, especially athletics and he did well in the decathlon. He lived in the small town where my father was born and my grandfather had been fire chief years before. He played badminton and that's how we met, at inter-club tournaments.

He seemed besotted, which I found surprising. I was self-conscious in those days, and my badminton skirt came down to my knees, not glamorous at all.

Our first date was to the movie *Jailhouse Rock*, which was playing at the theatre the teenagers referred to as the bughouse. Our courting years began with TC hitching rides to my home, or sometimes borrowing his father's car. He saved hard to buy a 1946 Austin 10 that we repainted with a cool stripe down the sides. I made faux leopard-skin covers for the dashboard to keep the sun off.

Entertainment was meagre: playing cards, movies or a river party on summer nights. I was sober in my habits. Beer came in quart bottles back then, and was warm before I could drink much. Several of my girlfriends indulged a little more, but nothing like some young ladies in recent times.

Our relationship moved quickly to a stage where I could envisage the possibility of starting a family, with this man as the father of my children. I was set on two boys and two girls and talked of that often, which didn't seem to put TC off. Could our relationship remain happy for the rest of my life? TC had no doubts at all: he had decided I was to be his wife, and he was persuasive.

I moved to his home town because he was doing a carpenter's apprenticeship. I applied for work at a home furniture and furnishings store. An excellent job that allowed me to further hone my interior decorating skills and become knowledgeable about fine china and silverware. I was learning something that interested me and I was only nineteen years of age.

The desire to have children while I was young was strong, but the general feeling of society then was that it was irresponsible to bring children into our world. Two arguments were put forward: the fear of nuclear war, and New Zealand's burgeoning population growth.

Given that New Zealand's population was only 2.6 million we decided to ignore that particular argument. I sensed it was important to build our family before moving on with my own career. We chanced the risk of a nuclear war, a good choice as it turned out.

We were married in February 1962 and moved to Paraparaumu. I was twenty years old. I turned twenty-one in November and delivered our first-born, in December. Twenty months later our son came along, so we had the pigeon pair. Parenting took a great deal of energy for a couple who had hardly allowed themselves time to grow up.

After a six-year gap we had two more daughters. All the babies were born in the same maternity hospital under the same matron. A woman to be admired, she kept a firm control on her ward, with the mothers as the central focus of her planning. Mothers stayed in hospital for two weeks after a first child was born, resting and doing exercises. Nourishing food was served to bring in the milk so mothers could breastfeed babies.

Some mothers chose not to breastfeed, but most were happy to avoid the extra work of sterilising baby bottles. There was little choice in baby formula, and my Plunket nurse advised weaning even young babies onto cow's milk, watered down, with brown sugar added.

I used the skills I learned at school and sewed all the children's clothes. Finally I had the pleasure of decorating my own beautiful home, the perfect house for a young family. TC was good at designing, and he planned a U-shaped house with no hallways. Everything, including my sewing cupboard, opened off a central room that became the children's play area. TC worked every weekend building the house for us, laying down each block and nailing each board. Our home grew slowly, making it all the more appreciated when we were able to move in.

I enjoyed being a mother and did a reasonable job, considering my parents weren't what one would call doting. They were more interested in providing a roof, a bed and encyclopaedias when we were older and letting us get on with it. I don't remember books in my childhood, except colouring books. We had Snakes and Ladders, Ludo and knuckle bones, but no stories to read.

I couldn't write my name when I went to school, but I was tricky and copied a girl with the same Christian name. A trick that got me told off, because my name was spelt differently from hers. I was born with a positive streak, so the growling didn't put me off learning. Instinctively I seemed to know I was the wise one, not my teacher.

Our marriage was happy; we had made the right choice. I raised the children and TC built houses in new developments. The 1970s were growth years, half-way between the recessions of the 60s and 80s. I was able to stay at home with the children, although I did manage a small job between the first two and the younger children. I spent my time wisely, studying high school accounting, and doing a correspondence course with Massey University. I studied world religions and psychology.

Our tenth anniversary came and went and then things began to change for our family. My father became ill with cancer in the early 1970s. Back then the medical specialists were reluctant to use the word cancer, and families either whispered the word or looked knowingly at each other and mouthed it. My father went through chemotherapy and radiation and yet he was never told what he was being treated for.

It turned out he had a tumour in his chest with tentacles that grew around his heart. The treatment was harsh and caused a great deal of pain. The radiation treatment was not filtered as it is today and more tissue than necessary was damaged. I believe the cure was worse than the disease.

We moved our family back to my hometown to be near my parents while my father was ill. During the three years it took for my Dad to surrender to the disease, we bought a house and a ten-acre block, the Kiwi dream back then – fatten a beast or two, find orphaned lambs for the children to feed and raise chickens for the eggs.

We had intended this to be our home after my father died, thinking we would be a support to my mother. However, it turned out my mother and I were not compatible, functioning from entirely different perspectives, and I had to admit this plan was imperfect. It wasn't difficult to sell the properties and begin again. We stuck a pin in a map and decided to move to Tauranga, a growing city with great potential for boating and fishing, and with good schools for the children.

In 1976, soon after our move, TC had a heart attack when he was only thirty-five. The strong athletic man we had all considered invincible had a weakness and the year that followed was traumatic. His doctors were unwilling to allow TC to return to building, saying the work was too heavy.

Money was short and applications for lighter work brought no relief. It is common for heart attack patients to go through a personality change. They become irritable, anxious and depressed, and this is made worse by financial worries. Prescribed medication for high blood pressure seemed to aggravate TC's symptoms further, including extreme fatigue and apathy.

The experience of watching how treatment for my father adversely affected him, and the reality of looking after a husband who had suffered considerable damage to his heart, led me to the study of alternative medicine. I had studied all my married life: interior design, accounting, world religions, psychology, music with Trinity College, journalism and nutrition. Taking on several more years of study wasn't daunting.

I believed I could learn how to treat circulatory and heart problems and the medical fraternity would co-operate with that choice. I was naïve. Even though there are many excellent choices when it comes to treating high blood pressure and blocked arteries, we would be discouraged from using these instead of drugs.

My husband had always been suspicious of using medical drugs, preferring to make lifestyle choices that kept the family in good health. It was easy for him to opt for the natural route. Over the next thirty years, he survived six heart attacks, recovering rapidly and living a fit and healthy lifestyle between each attack. We travelled extensively and, best of all, he was able to walk his three daughters down the aisle on their wedding day.

The battle with the doctors and their insistence that he take medical drugs was ongoing and at times distressing for me. TC, on the other hand, never had any doubts about his decision. I remember one time he was in hospital following an attack and his doctor gave him a good telling-off.

"If you had been taking the medical drugs we prescribed," he raged, "you would not be in this hospital bed today."

TC leaned forward in his bed and waved his arm along the ward full of heart attack patients.

"So all these patients stopped their medication, did they?"

On this same visit to hospital, his blood pressure was elevated even though he was taking the medically-prescribed drug. This meant he would not be given a clearance to go home. He encouraged me to return to our house and collect his supplements. Within five hours he was discharged with normal blood pressure. He continued to take his vitamins and the herbal hawthorn formula he had researched and chosen because he knew they worked for him.

We bought another lifestyle block in Te Puna, this time to give TC a job he could work at his own pace. He cut down extensive shelter belts and removed the kiwi fruit vines for our new venture, breeding emu. We believed these were an economical use of land because a pair of emu could lay up to forty eggs at a time. The chicks only had to be raised to two years old, when they provided a good quantity of low fat protein that was both tender and delicious to eat.

We enjoyed the challenge of raising our first emu from tiny chicks. Cute, striped and fluffy, they became our pets and we named them. In the early days of breeding the eggs were hatched in incubators, but we allowed one pair to raise the clutch in the paddock. Legs, the male emu, so-named because he was tall, raised his fourteen young without any problems, a joy to watch.

Taking care of the animals gave me a chance to get out in the sunshine on the weekends. I drove home after working inside at the clinic all week to our pristine garden paradise. I carried feed to each paddock while my pets pecked at my hair and buttons.

I had built a busy clinic over the years and noticed an alarming number of my patients suffered from low blood sugar and anxiety. I took an interest in finding how to alleviate the varied symptoms this caused. I began to realise that holistic health care was more than knowing which vitamins, minerals or herbs were traditionally used for a particular illness.

Popping natural pills was not the total answer to health problems. Patients did respond well with fewer side effects, but it is also important to get to the cause of any illness, and offer natural ways of recovery.

I continued my studies, firstly a diploma in osteopathy, and then in cranial osteopathy. Spinal misalignments interfere with neuro-messages to the body's organs, so asthma, diabetes and constipation are a few of the many symptoms that can occur.

I studied clinical hypnosis, which proved helpful for extreme stress, addictions and phobias. Unnatural fears can be restricting. One patient became extremely fearful of dogs and was reluctant to go for walks in case she met an unfriendly animal. After hypnosis, she took a Staffordshire terrier into her home rather than allow him to be shot by his owner.

Applied kinesiology, the study of movement, was another good tool and included many other useful tests that help in diagnosing food sensitivities and clearing emotional problems.

Astrology might seem a strange choice to make next, but I had noticed a pattern in the symptoms suffered by patients. I would have a run of patients book in with diabetes or asthma, and began to question why that was.

Sometimes several patients on a given day would arrive clutching their neck or walking like a banana with acute lower back pain. Was this merely coincidence or was it was the pull of the moon?

TC always considered the moon when he went

fishing and we all know how the moon affects the tide. Given humans are mostly water I figured it was worth investigation.

This study proved to be the most interesting of all. The moon does play a part in our health, but in a much more complex manner than I had thought, a story all its own. Suffice to say this became another useful tool in the clinic.

The trigger for most pain and illness comes from a stressor or situation that is difficult for the patient to deal with. In other words, stress, and not only the stress itself, but how the patient responds physically, emotionally and mentally to that stress or situation.

One of the early examples in my clinical career was a man with severe shoulder pain. The patient had not suffered any apparent physical trauma, but his range of motion was restricted and he had been in pain for several months.

After a couple of treatments that did little to change the symptoms, I asked. "What are you holding on to?"

The patient was instantly able to tell me.

"My wife died seven months ago and I visit the cemetery every day. I can't get used to being without her."

This admission focused the patient on his need to let go. He still visited her graveside; he still missed his wife but the pain in his shoulders disappeared within days.

Medical drugs are convenient and, generally, people just want to get rid of symptoms quickly. It is important to remember that when immigrants landed in the 1840s, they used willow bark successfully for pain and fever, and hawthorn was the medicine used to balance blood pressure right up until World War II.

Maori had many herbal medicines of their own, which we could have incorporated. Since 1942 – less than one lifetime – the pharmaceutical industry as we know it has become the normal method of treatment and natural medicine is considered to be quackery, something to be warned against.

The use of post-war medicine increased quickly with the discovery of antibacterial drugs, insulin, and antihypertensive drugs. These, along with the contraceptive pill, seemed like miracle cures and required little patient compliance. In the 1980s, when I began my naturopathy practice, the pharmaceutical industry was well established.

One of my first patients came to me with several complaints, but she was taking no medical pills because of allergies to the drugs. I can remember thinking what a challenge this could be. I discovered it to be the opposite. Lifestyle changes and appropriate mineral and herbal treatments worked quickly and efficiently for her and gave her peace of mind. Staying disease-free does not depend on chemicals. Over the years, I have treated many people who have chosen not to become dependent on medical drugs, using them for short periods only.

With the scientific advances being made in diagnosis and treatments that include light and sound therapy, future generations will have more and better choices so that debilitating illnesses may well disappear.

<h1 style="text-align:center">Chapter 25</h1>

Post-war. Steam runs headlong into cyber
1945, and one hundred years since the Shadbolts were transported in shame to serve time on Norfolk Island; one hundred years since the Wallaces joined the army to escape starvation in Ireland; one hundred and five years since the Breitmeyers left on a leaky boat from France, and the Pawsons sailed from Yorkshire, England.

These stories are almost forgotten because the world has languished under the strain of two world wars. Fond memories of the years before the wars were lost in the silence the soldiers now preferred.

Post-war everything changed forever, and with ever increasing speed. The wars had forced mankind to find new ways to kill and maim, new guns, new machines, new vehicles, new aeroplanes, new and faster ships to make the world a smaller place.

Food became packaged to feed the army;

cigarettes were produced to keep soldiers calm in the trenches. Surgeons learned better and quicker ways to cut into injured flesh and remove body parts. Drug companies invented pills to deaden the pain of men's bodies and minds. Prosthetic limbs and anaesthetics used in surgery were improved.

World War I began these changes with the need for better communication. The runners, flags, pigeons, lamps and dispatch riders were no use to men in aeroplanes. Radio communication was refined and a speaker incorporated in the pilot's helmet so they could hear above the noise of the plane. Rather than pocket watches, the men on the ground used wrist-watches which could be accessed more quickly to co-ordinate operations.

The injuries of this war required an absorbent wad to be developed to adequately dress horrific wounds. Nurses, many of them young women from New Zealand, discovered another and more lasting use for this item and began to wear them as sanitary pads.

The need to find a better metal for gun barrels began the rapid development of stainless steel, which was also used for surgical equipment. Many other useful items were invented such as: the zip to fasten clothes, teabags, paper hankies and daylight saving.

The ballpoint pen, which didn't need filling from an inkwell, made its debut between the wars. American pilots during World War II popularised them, by demonstrating how much better they worked at high altitudes.

World War II brought to the fore some ordinary, and some extremely out of the ordinary inventions. The dynamo torch, jerry cans, duct tape, jet engines, and the production of 2.3 million doses of penicillin, saving 15-20 percent of casualties who would have died from infection.

Radar, and with that, the microwave transmitter that later would lead to the microwave oven. The first computer, *Colossus*, helped push the development of the modern PC. And perhaps the most controversial discovery of all, the potential power stored in an atom to provide nuclear power, and the worst of all evils, the atomic bomb.

The speed of change continued, with the use of electricity, production lines, and even faster communications. Travel, music, as well as the ever-changing post-war fashions where hems moved from ankle to knee and down again, up to the thigh with the mini and down again with the midi.

The men who served in these wars spoke little of the horrors they had seen, encouraging their children to make the most of this burgeoning new world, and look forward to the future. A future that introduced the concept of consumerism, with an amazing range of electrical appliances and toys for both young and old.

Temptations tirelessly promoted by the *Madmen of Madison Square*, with advertising campaigns that could coax or dupe even the most discerning to buy, buy, buy.

Consumers became besotted with refrigerators, musical synthesizers, the pill, transistor radios, hula hoops and Barbie dolls in the Fifties.

Television and Valium were the favourites in the Sixties.

Ping-pong, video games, post-it pads, laser and jet printers and cell phones, the size of a brick, in the Seventies.

User-friendly computers by Windows, 3-D video games and Cabbage Patch Kids. Digital cell phones that changed communication in ways manufacturers didn't anticipate made their appearance in the Eighties. The cell phone was designed as a useful tool for businesses, yet soon it became obvious it was going to be so much more and sales rocketed. Families texted home to say they'd be late, friends sent texts to locate mates at rugby matches.

The Nineties began with the World Wide Web and ended with Viagra. (Could there be a connection?)

In the year 2000, millennium celebrations that cost millions of dollars filled TV screens around the world, sweeping from New Zealand to London and ending in Samoa a little over twenty-five hours later. Firework displays, souvenirs and patriotic symbols to inspire hope for a new and improved twenty-first century.

Would the wars of past decades cease? Would work be available to all, would wealth be fairly distributed? No. The wars continued, only the location changing, and jobs dwindled as the mechanisation and automation of factories, farms, hospitals and offices took its toll.

By 2008 the global financial crash stole the houses of the young and the retirement savings of the old. Governments bailed out banks who had lent money to naïve clients who had no hope of keeping up the payments. New Zealand lost trade in Europe where many countries suffered a liquidity crisis. Trade deals had to be made with China and business increased generally in the Pacific.

Many of the jobs created in the previous century had been in the food industry, growing meat and vegetables, and such jobs are the most vulnerable to the changing world of mechanisation and robotics. The farms of the future will boast tractors that drive themselves, milk bots for milking the cows and drones for delivery.

The farm workers are out of work. Does this sound at

In the future all low-paid jobs such as cleaning, serving food and beverages, garment manufacturing, data entry, and postal services will be done by machines.

Sweatshops have always been with us, but globalisation and chains of cheap department stores started a new round in Third World countries. Some argued these countries needed the financial boost this brought, but many grew rich from the misery of others. Robots will put an end to sweatshops because there will be no financial gain from human servitude.

And it will not only be low-paid positions under threat. Teachers will become obsolete with Google and other search engines for research and online, interactive subject teaching. If a teenager is unable for some reason to attend school long-term currently, the curriculum is already available on their PC.

In the investment industry advisers will be superseded by carefully-programmed computer analyses. Modern medicine has seen job casualties already with 1,000 robot-assisted surgeries in the year 2000 and 570,000 in 2014.

Those affected by the rapid changes of both globalisation and technology around the world are speaking out and demonstrating their dissatisfaction at the ballot box. The surprise exit vote of Britain from the European Union (EU) on 23rd June 2016 after forty-three years' membership is only the beginning.

Even though both Northern Ireland and Scotland voted strongly to remain in Europe, the population of Britain made a controversial decision to exit. A time of adjustment will be needed to unravel the impact on New Zealand. What will this mean for New Zealand's exports of meat, dairy and wine?

The history of the EU goes back nearly seventy years. During the 1950s, the European coal and steel community formed a six-country alliance that included Belgium, France, West Germany, Italy, Luxembourg and the Netherlands. These nations became the forerunner to the Common Market. Britain didn't make application until 1961, but was vetoed by the French Government in 1963 and again on its second application in 1967.

Further negotiations for British membership began in 1969 and on 1st January 1973 Britain was able to join along with Denmark and Ireland. Once Britain was established in the EU, the implications were obvious for New Zealand, rather like a divorce from the homeland, where adjustments, as with any divorce must be made and losses are inevitable.

Slowly privileges for New Zealand passport holders were reduced, although young and not-so-young continued to take advantage of the overseas experience – 'the big O.E' – by living and working in the UK where they were popular employees.

The history of France and Germany has also affected New Zealand, beginning with two World Wars. More recently the shift to substantial trade deals with other EU members after Britain joined. The Brexit turn-around and a threat by France of following Britain will bring a fresh round of negotiations.

New Zealand has been proactive and extremely successful in finding alternative export markets and was the first to reach a free market agreement in 2008 with China, the world's largest economy.

Opportunities in the USA market had been scarce because of the nuclear-free stand New Zealand took in banning nuclear ships from our ports. The Disarmament and Arms Control Act of 1987 makes the territorial sea, land and airspace of New Zealand nuclear-free zones. New Zealand showed the world that even a small country can stand up for its beliefs and build a productive system of trade.

The trade freeze that America put on New Zealand has thawed in recent years with a visit from President Clinton in 2010 making the USA our third largest trading partner. America now uses more cordial terms to describe our relationship, such as 'deep and longstanding friendship.' This new warmth may reflect the focus on the Pacific as a major player in the world economy rather than forgiveness for our audacity. Whether our deep and longstanding friendship status remains in place is still to be seen with Trump as America's President-Elect.

The 2016 Australian election was extremely close. Voters were confused and blame spread wide: it's the older generation, it's the poor, and it's the uneducated. Is New Zealand learning lessons from the mismanagement of the last twenty to thirty years? Globalisation has caused an ever-increasing gap between the rich and poor, unnoticed it would appear until it is too late and those affected started to fight back.

America saw fit to vote with what has been labelled a white-lash because it was mainly white male voters who hit back at the establishment by voting for a business man with no political experience. These were men struggling to maintain a moderate existence, and believing in change of any kind as their only hope for a better future.

This is an age when men can make more money than they can possibly spend by thinking up 'stuff' for the eager consumers to buy. The more people that buy these trinkets the richer the makers get. Making money from the global market will become unachievable when consumers are without jobs, and therefore without money.

To ignore this problem would be foolhardy. If the dissatisfied masses don't get what they consider a fair share, they might loot, rob or revolt.

Governments may already be using artificial intelligence (AI) software, and its developing sophistication, at an alarmingly speedy rate. AI will be programmed to think like humans and make predictions, assisting agencies, corporate and government departments to respond to and work out solutions to economic, fiscal and social issues as they arise.

Some state with certainty that over half the jobs of the twentieth century will no longer exists when the twenty-first century ends. Remaining jobs will have titles that include one or more of the following words: system analysts, software, engineer, technical, network, wireless, database, robotics, telecommunications, applications, security, web design, artificial intelligence or information.

New Zealand was the home chosen by the pioneers of the 1800s, not only the Scottish, English, French and German families whose stories we've glimpsed, but others who have settled and helped to build a culturally diverse and successful country. How will our country address the rapid changes in world trade and, more vitally, the cyber age we're heading into with ever-increasing speed? Will it lead the way?

In 2016 the World Economic Forum report on global information technology listed New Zealand as the seventeenth best-prepared nation for future digital technology. Singapore was number one followed by Finland and Sweden. Now is the time to be planning ahead. There's no point in arguing over trivia or being stuck in steam-age thinking. The country is crying out for a solution to the cyber revolution.

With job losses, recreation of all kinds will be an increasing part of future living. With fewer working hours and a higher number of the unemployed, there will be a rising demand for leisure time activities: entertaining and being entertained, sports and fitness, the appreciation of fine art and good books to fill our days.

Travel will be easier, quicker and cheaper, with holidaymakers making favourite destinations even more crowded. The growth of virtual reality will allow us to take a never to be forgotten tour of the Louvre or Musee d'Orsay. There one can spend the hours studying the *Mona Lisa* or Paul Gauguin's amazing use of colour. Would it be prudent for our youth to be engaging now with the arts, sports, film-making?

The basic need is for a decent income to buy food, shelter, education and a certain amount of leisure and pleasure, and that's not going away. If the jobs are gone, the way society functions will become outmoded. There will be no one who can afford the phones, the cars, the gadgets. The economists, humanitarians, churches, politicians, criminologists, local bodies, educational institutions and health providers need to be planning now.

Chapter 26

Generations

Since the generation that fought in the world wars for our freedom – *the generation of the hero* – each generation has lived through events causing at least some stereotyping.

The silent generation of the 30s and 40s. This now ageing generation whose parents fought in one or often in two of the world wars, lived their childhood years in a time of scarcity, especially following the Great Depression. They have been witnesses from the very beginning of the technological race, but cannot be relied upon to utilise technology to find solutions.

The Baby Boomers of the 50s and early 60s, who as the name suggests are plentiful, because they are the post-war babies, are said by some to be rapidly becoming part of the problem. They have either made it by now, with their negative hedging investments, and are able to take care of themselves as they grow older, or they are a potential drain on society.

This generation tends to gather together, happy to attend meetings and more likely to carry banners of protest than roll up their sleeves and fight. A large percentage will vote for the government they believe will be best for them rather than for a party.

The X generation; mid-60s to mid-80s, are part of the awakening Consciousness Revolution, shedding light on human rights. They lived through the era of assassinations: J.F. Kennedy, Robert Kennedy and Martin Luther King. In their childhood years, they watched the Vietnam War unfold on TV over the dinner table. These were the Cold War years when the Berlin Wall was still standing.

One in four of this generation who were in a relationship did not legally marry. They understand values, civil rights and equality of gender and race. This generation began the youth culture and attended Woodstock, or in New Zealand's case the Great Ngaruawahia Music Festival. A generation that may lead the way for caring and sharing in the future.

The Millennial or Y (why) generation; mid-80s to 2000 may well put on virtual reality headsets and disappear for years. Hopefully, this will not be the case because theirs is the generation that will be most affected by increasing job losses. Recognise them serving in your local bar to pay for their education, a friendly and helpful group.

They are less inclined to vote, but more inclined to complain that things are not going their way, understandably blaming the Baby Boomers for depleting resources.

The New Silent or Homeland generation; 2000 to ? Their childhood years were spent during the 2008 recession and the war on terror. They will have the benefit of rapidly-developing technology at their disposal. And, at the least, should be able to plan their future and adjust as they watch the Millennials succeed or fail as the case may be.

Even though they are young they are aware of globalisation, global warming, sweat shops and the need to be discerning when purchasing products.

A brief synopsis of some of the new technology demonstrates a little of what will be available to the younger generations as they grow to adulthood.

The Hyper-loop, designed to move freight or passengers along a track at super high speeds. Trains designed earlier have to travel in straight lines or with minimal curves to keep the containers on the tracks, but in countries where there are great distances to transport freight, this is not necessarily a disadvantage for now.

Driverless cars have become almost commonplace in our thinking, with many companies working to improve design and safety with inventions such as car-to-car communications, a wireless technology to make driverless cars safer.

Work began in 1990 on the Hypersonic Reactive Engines, designed for rocket style aircraft that could be carrying passengers by 2036. The craft would travel at five times the speed of sound after a vertical take-off then land miles away from lift-off in a few hours. Nanotechnology; the implications of this new technology are vast.

Kai Wu has written, 'Imagine a technology so powerful that it will allow such feats as desktop manufacturing, cellular repair, artificial intelligence, inexpensive space travel, clean abundant energy, environmental restoration; a technology so portable that everyone can reap its benefits - which will radically change our economic and political systems - and so imminent that most of us will see its impact within our lifetimes.'

Nano-Architecture using tiny lattice-like structures will be a fraction of the weight of commonly used materials in architecture.

Liquid Biopsy, fast DNA sequencing machines to screen for cancer.

The IBM supercomputer named Watson helps diagnose cancer four times more accurately than doctors.

Companies like Tricorder are developing devices that diagnose in seconds from sensors or photos.

Brain Organoids are a method of growing brain cells to aid the study of brain dysfunction.

Digital Genome allows your health care to be decided from the genic-code information on a USB.

Cultured meat or lab meat grown in the laboratory. The agricultural land used for raising cattle is thirty percent of the agricultural land surface and the emissions of CO2 would be reduced. An alternative protein made from insects is already available.

Mega scale desalination plants already operate in Israel, and the need for water is growing daily. The CEO of Nestlé seems to believe corporate ownership of water will serve us better than the free supplies we're used to, so desalination may prove the only way to survive?

The Mini-Drone or RoboBee is developing extremely quickly to become a valuable search and rescue tool after earthquakes and landslips. (A smart wine bottle that keeps wine fresh for thirty days, though it might need to be a larger bottle, I'm thinking).

Distributed manufacturing is where raw materials will be decentralised and manufactured nearer to the consumer. Digital information can be sent via the web rather than physical products over roads or rails, and raw materials may be sourced locally, with a saving in energy and transportation and safer roads.

Over a period of ten years 3D printers reduced in price from thousands of dollars to a few hundred dollars; they are one hundred times faster, and print anything from shoes and space station parts to tall buildings.

Asimo has been developed over thirty years to become a versatile and useful robot. It can walk and run up to nine kilometres per hour – not an easy task – with sensors maintaining a body's posture comparable with the action. *Asimo* can kick a soccer ball directly to a team member.

The Kokomo Company is developing the Actroid (actor-android) that will closely resemble a human being, with character and warmth. During the development of this android, Takeshi Mita discovered there was a considerable difference in the expectations of men and women when it came to the physical appearance of the Actroid. Women preferred a more smartly dressed model that showed intelligence, rather than a droid in a mini skirt.

Researchers at Leibniz University in Hannover, Germany, are developing an artificial robot nervous system so that robots can feel pain. This would allow robots to identify pain so that they respond quickly to avoid damaging themselves.

The US Marine Corp *Petman,* which looks like a cross between a dog and a small horse, can gallop and bound along at efficient speeds, while the NASA *Curiosity Rover* meanders around picking up samples, like the trooper it is.

The Dunedin Multidisciplinary Health and Development Study (DMHDS) is the longest ever study of its kind beginning with babies born in 1972-1973, following them through to adulthood forty-four years later. The study continues and the information is being used all over the world in an effort to improve the lives of children and to pinpoint trends and crucial turning points in human behaviour.

Mark Zuckerberg and his team have launched the first solar aeroplane. *The Aquila* drone, with the wingspan of an airliner, is designed to fly non-stop for three months and will use lasers to beam down Internet access to remote areas. Education will be available to those who do not have contact with the outside world and allow them to see things they never thought possible. They will, however, need money to take full advantage of what the world has to offer.

The CERN hadron collider, costing nine billion dollars, is situated on the border of France and Switzerland, and invokes all sorts of responses as it sends sub-atomic particles at the speed of light along a twenty-seven kilometre circuit to smash into each other.

CERN also has an interest in discovering the elusive particles or 'whatever' responsible for dark matter and dark energy using the atom smasher. No-one seems to have much idea of what the consequence will be, but the experiment continues, though British physicist, Stephen Hawking, has voiced warnings.

Elon Musk announced in a recent presentation that his SpaceX's vision is for humans to be building a city on the surface of Mars. Preparations will be starting as soon as possible.

Epilogue

The wars did not end.

Generation X are the new politicians now, but even though they learned how to cope during the difficult years of the global financial crash, they cannot find a solution to the poverty and violence.

The peacemakers put forward solutions, but there was always something standing in the way and delaying the implementation of new ideas. They thought to bring an end to the greed – sharing resources fairly – to enable the purchasing power of the poor to keep the new cyber-industrial age buoyant.

Technology improved beyond all expectations unfortunately, the warmongers had more money to spend than the humanitarians. The risk of war was greater now than at any other time, with every nation owning nuclear capabilities.

The threat to humankind had never been so real. Escape to another planet became the only option to ensure the human race did not annihilate itself and the Earth forever.

A civilisation on Mars could begin anew, discarding the tangled web of social injustice, and building a society of equal rights.

The lessons learned about global warming from Earth would be invaluable for warming the atmosphere of Mars and reducing cosmic radiation.

The colonists would be sent in groups and infrastructure could grow slowly as needs were met.

2040

Cousins Hamiora, Will, Simone, and Rose stood together, strapped into their vertical landing seats as the spacecraft touched down with a jolt on the dusty red surface. They were among a group of one hundred about to begin a life very different from what they were used to.

The spaceships carrying colonisers to Mars had been orbiting Earth waiting for the optimal time to begin the five month journey.

The best opportunity for travel to Mars comes around every two years when the planet is almost in opposition to Earth. This is when the space ships get ready to begin the long journey. Three thousand more colonisers will be following this first landing during the relatively short colonisation period.

The years of preparation were over and permanent colonisation was about to become a reality, with each traveller chosen for particular abilities: Hamiora, a communications specialist; Simone, a journalist and author; Will, a top-level athlete and exercise expert with qualifications in the treatment of sports and physical injuries; and Rose, a scientist and inventor.

Of equal importance was their genetic makeup. Gravity was still low on Mars so the inhabitants needed to come from a genetic pool that did not suffer from extreme bone loss. All new settlers had to undergo a rigorous exercise programme during the five-month space flight to maintain strong bones and muscle.

The three thousand newcomers were to play an important role in developing Mars for the generations who would follow them. They would release gases that would slowly warm the planet, build a city filled with amenities, and set up socially-based councils to ensure a community with equal rights. All this to be ready for the next intake in two years' time.

The colonists peered out of the portholes into the dense red dust. The building that would soon be their home could still be seen through the haze. Warning lights were flashing and there was a sense of urgency as residents came to help them disembark.

"Follow the red line, and move as quickly as you can. We want to get you settled before this storm worsens."

The cousins moved forward with a sense of anticipation mixed with the fear that comes with a commitment so far from reality that it is almost paralysing. Questions crowded their mind that only time would answer.

"I'm Frank," said the older man who was assigned to welcome the newcomers. He handed out maps as he explained, "You will be in the East Wing. Find your names on the door of your suite. You will notice all the wings link back to this central core. This is where you will meet for almost all activities".

"You will get your orders from here, your meals will be served here and some of you will be in charge of developing our entertainment areas further along the passageway. I suggest you go to your rooms and unpack ready for the Commander's official welcome in one hour."

Hamiora led the way along the corridor where the white paint and lack of adornment created a sterile effect, but which did reflect the wall lights that had been dimmed to save power. He searched for their names.

"Here we go; these are our rooms. Will, you and I are in here and Simone and Rose, you are in the room opposite. Wow! We have a porthole. Nothing but dust right now, but better than a blank wall, and the dust will settle soon, I hope."

"It might or it might not. Sometimes the storms go on for weeks," suggested Rose, who had a particular interest in the weather, the atmosphere and the growing of food in harsh conditions. "But I like your room, guys. Better than I imagined and the bathroom is five-star."

"Let's check out our room," suggested Simone. "It had better be as good as this. Then we'd best unpack and be on time for the Commander's welcome."

Both rooms were exactly the same, and this wing was plainly for singletons.

The Commander was young like most residents in the city. A techno wiz on Earth, his broad education included human behaviour and leadership. He welcomed the new settlers, apologising about the dust storm.

"You'll learn to take them in your stride," he assured them, then proceeded with a warning.

"We are going to be sealed in for some time. This is a bad storm and we need to conserve power, water and food. I suggest you imagine you are in the

Antarctic for the next couple of weeks and ration accordingly. It will be a good opportunity to get to know your fellow workers and those of you here to work on entertainment will gain a feel of its importance to us."

"The journo could put out a memo on what's going on behind the scenes on Earth and some good old-fashioned fiction would be appreciated. Your first meal will be served soon then it is best to retire to your cabins. Use the magnetic charging torches. They take some effort to charge, but will allow you to relax about using lights because you are conserving the main power supply. Meet here tomorrow and you will be assigned a helper to get you started."

The food was no surprise because Rose had helped develop the steaks and sausages produced from a mixture of insects and vegetable protein. There was no tomato sauce; in fact, no sauce at all. The vegetables, colourful and nourishing, were from the internal hydroponic garden because the outside gardens could not be reached during the storm.

It would be part of Rose's duties to build up compost to add to the dehydrated peat they'd brought on the ship. This would allow a greater variety of plants to be grown although the soil on Mars was surprisingly fertile.

The mealtime was shorter than usual to save

power for lighting, so there was only a brief period to introduce themselves to the land crew before the cousins retired to the room allocated to the men. They sat and talked while they charged their magnetic torches, tipping them backwards and forwards in a steady rhythm that automatically converted the kinetic energy into electric energy to be stored in a hybrid energy storage cell.

The white LED-bulbs were bright enough to read by and comforting to the four as they faced their first night on a different planet from family and friends left behind on Earth. The dust storm raged outside the window, intensifying the sense of isolation they were experiencing.

"I'm pleased we all came together. I'm not sure I could have done this on my own."

Rose, the youngest of the cousins, felt her eyes moisten and her voice waver. She was close to her family including aunties and uncles, preferring them to be within travelling distance when she wanted to visit.

"I agree," said Will.

Neither Will nor Hamiora had siblings so they had learned to manage on their own, relying on their cousins for moral support when things got tough.

"I wonder if this is what it felt like to be an early settler in New Zealand."

They'd taken a keen interest in their pioneering

ancestry and shared the same adventurous nature as those who had helped build New Zealand.

"If I remember correctly they landed during a cold and rainy week with only a tent for shelter."

"Yes, they did," Simone agreed. "They must have felt what we feel now. Hope, excitement – some fear, and fatigue. It took them as long to reach New Zealand from Europe as it has taken us to get to Mars." She yawned. "Let's get some sleep. Things always look better after a night's rest."

The morning brought a return of the optimistic energy that had brought them to volunteer for Mars. They met early and went on a tour of their surroundings. The walls in the communal lounge were decorated with framed photos displaying the early days of Mars exploration. Pride of place was reserved for *Mariner 4*, the seventy-five-year old veteran that had reached Mars on 14th of July 1965. The photo showed the craft surrounded by the twenty-one photos it had sent back to earth. These presented an untypical view of the planet, giving the impression the surface of Mars was similar to the moon.

The display moved on ten years with photos of *Vikings 1* and *2* and their landers, which had sent back to Earth 50,000 photos for examination. These showed a different scene – one that demonstrated that Mars was not at all like the moon.

The photos taken during the 1990s recorded the era of the 'Better Faster Cheaper' projects that made such significant discoveries. The Mars Global Surveyor gave ten years of service, mapping the planet from pole to pole.

The *Mars Odyssey,* launched in March 2001, became a record-breaker with the landing rovers, *Spirit* and *Opportunity*, covering many kilometres on the surface. The ill-fated stationary lander, *Mars Phoenix,* that landed on 25th May 2008 made the exciting discovery of water ice beneath the surface.

Sadly, the harsh Mars winter damaged the solar panels and communication was lost all too soon.

A more powerful *Curiosity* landed at Gale Crater in 2012, and made other major discoveries such as methane gas on the surface and organic compounds considered the building blocks of life. The photographic display told an amazing story of perseverance and faith that made possible the permanent colonisation of Mars in 2040.

For four years the first wave of settlers had been battling a hostile environment. They had made it possible for the new group to begin changes that would make the planet more habitable for the larger migration to follow. Attention from now on would focus on the health and well-being of the citizens. Better food choices, versatile additions to the entertainment centres, and improved communication systems.

The time spent examining the photos set the scene for the first day in their new home. Assistants arrived to show the new recruits around. Will was taken by Izzy to check out the exercise facilities. He would then make a start on his two-hour personal rehabilitation programme to assist with his recovery after the long flight.

The gymnasium was poorly equipped, with only the essentials to maintain health among the residents. There were rock climbing walls and a couple of Lower Body Negative Pressure devices (LBNP). The negative pressure device is a treadmill encased in a chamber which the user seals around the lower body. The air is sucked from the chamber creating negative pressure, similar to the Earth's gravity.

The value to the user is multiple: improved bone density, an aerobic workout that reduced muscle atrophy and increased blood flow bringing calcium to the lower extremities.

Will was pleased to find a row of vibrating plates that provided low-frequency vertical oscillations that could be set between 30 and 90 Hz oscillations, and used for shorter periods of ten to twenty minutes twice daily. Other than these devices there were yoga and Pilate mats, and rubber stretching bands.

Izzy had other duties to attend to.

"I'll leave you with a programme and you can make any changes you think would suit you better."

"Ok. I'll work something out for my cousins as well. We could swap notes in a week or so on how they compare with your usual programme if you like."

"Good thinking."

Simone and Hamiora were taken by Chanelle to the communications area. This was a more sophisticated setup than they had expected, with access to Earth and messages relayed within a few days of them being sent. Hamiora was shown the plans for enlarging the centre, then Chanelle suggested he get his exercise programme started.

"You might as well go with him, Simone. That's more important than a newspaper right now. You can print us a brief on your trip later then get started for real tomorrow."

"I do need to do my exercise."

Simone screwed up her nose.

"Though I'm not that partial to time in the gym. Where can I meet you if I have questions about the news items?"

"I'll see you in the lunch room or you can message

me any time."

Rose could not visit the garden area because of the storm, so Geo introduced her to the science team and she was given some data to read in her own time.

Rose was a tall, strong woman who had suffered only minimum bone loss on the flight, but she still needed to work through her personal program. Exercise was not only essential for the maintenance of physical health, but also uplifted mood as serotonin and endorphins entered the blood stream.

The cousins felt more in tune with their new environment as they made their way to the canteen. Lunch was relaxed and longer than last night's meal because much of the work was suspended by the storm.

This gave the new settlers time to get to know their fellow citizens. They noticed the original members shared their knowledge and listened intently to what the cousins had to say, glad of any opportunity to explore new ways to improve life on Mars.

The storm lasted another week. By now most of the crew were anxious to inspect any damage outside.

Rose didn't have to travel far to the gardens and was about to get her first look at her transport. She was scheduled to meet at the docking bay, where she could see short distance transport vehicles parked against the wall of the main building.

Her assistant, Geo, explained that the vehicles for transport to the garden were pressurised so they could walk through the connecting tunnel and board from there.

"The vehicle is easy to drive, and will become your best friend, transporting you backwards and forward as you do your experiments.

"This is great, saves time suiting up. I guess you have expectations for a more varied diet?"

Geo nodded her head and licked her lips, smiling.

"You could say that. We're bored with the present choices, I must admit. But we can't complain. At least we've had fresh vegetables to add variety to the freeze-dried formulas. None of the initial crew members had great culinary skills. To stay healthy was the most we expected. Now it's time to branch out a little. I'd give anything for some fresh bread and honey."

"I'll be working on that for sure," grinned Rose.

Rose realised that her work here would be rewarding and the crew would appreciate a range of tasty menus. That's what she'd been working on back on Earth, coming up with some talented ideas to improve food supplies for the space station astronauts. Similar techniques could be used here.

Chris, a vehicle mechanic, met up with Hamiora, Will and Simone to suggest they take a spin in a larger space exploration vehicle (SEV).

"It will be an orientation trip and to get you out and about for a break.'

Hamiora had plenty to do inside, but was not about to refuse such an offer. It was useful for Simone to take a good look around and write some columns to send back to Earth. Will was interested in how he could improve recreation on the planet. An inside golf putting course was already in use, and Will was keen to start some extravehicular activities to add variety.

"I'm planning to build a golf course that will be one big sand bunker," he explained. "No greens or water hazards, but the wind storms form these high ridges, which will be a bit of a challenge. The good part is our hooks and slices will improve by one hundred times per second and our drives will go three times further. A different game from golf on Earth and a good social event, I can visualise you two, kangaroo-hopping along a course three times larger than you're used to."

"I'm in," Hamiora assured him, "and what about some snowboarding?"

"Not as silly as it sounds," said Will. "We can bring back some dry ice and shape them into boards. The boards slide dangerously fast down the bigger slopes because when the ice hits the warmer sand it releases CO_2 that forms a layer of gas between the sledge and the sand so even a slight gradient gives an exciting ride."

"I'm not doing that then." Simone wanted to make that clear straight away. "But I'll be there, that's for sure, taking pics for my blog, 'The Marscodex'. You're going to need some serious help with all this."

"I am. But don't worry. There'll be hundreds of new residents arriving in the next week or so and plenty of robots to take on basic tasks. This will be the biggest population intake ever so we'll be making big changes during the next two years. Mars will be popular real estate when we've finished with it."

It wasn't long before workers were constructing pods for reading rooms, a library and TV rooms. The greenhouses were enlarged and fitted with solar panels. Maintenance teams were busy updating and upgrading the original buildings and equipment. Courses were set up to teach everything from art to philosophy. The entire workforce became researchers, adding new information and ideas to get the most out of every project.

The governing of the city was left entirely to the community with experienced personnel in a particular field leading and teaching the others any number of multiple tasks. Job sharing was encouraged because it brought variety into each day's activities.

No carrot and stick tactics because everyone worked hard to make their city the best it could be. The rewards came from improving conditions whenever and wherever possible. There was no need for money because all needs were met and each got an equal share.

Two years passed quickly for the cousins. They were given the opportunity to return to Earth, but none of them wanted to leave the work they were doing. The four of them had made an impact on the residents' everyday lives.

Simone's novels reflected the amazing planet that had become home for her, and were top sellers on Earth, making readers dream of taking part in the Mars adventure she depicted.

Hamiora improved communications considerably. Contact between Mars and Earth, which many still called 'home' was quick, and reception clear, almost like being in the same room. Hamiora and Simone jointly created web clips to document this phase of colonisation for the next generations.

Rose and Will had become favourites with all the settlers because good food and entertainment were what they looked for at day's end and days off.

The crew members who were returning to Earth were about to leave. Hamiora and Will shook hands and promised to stay in touch. It was hard to say goodbye to friends who'd become closer than family. Simone and Rose hugged them close, blinking back tears as they wished them a safe journey. Some of the original Mars Project crew were leaving today, among them Chris, Channelle, Geo and Izzy.

These brave volunteers had not known if they'd survive in this alien environment when they first arrived. They had paved the way for mass colonisation, working without the luxuries added over the last two years.

"Who's for coffee?" asked Rose "I hate goodbyes, and it's worse when you know this may be the last time we see these guys face-to-ace."

"Sure is. Let's go and talk about our plans for the next two years."

Simone had her time mapped out already.

The cousins would have no trouble finding things to do in the coming years. The next group of settlers would be arriving over the next few days and expansion was needed in every department. New pods, new vehicles, larger gardens, more space for activities.

News from Earth continued to be disturbing. Stories of wars and terrorism hadn't changed. Water was scarce and food crops were failing because the soil was depleted. Many parts of the world have become a dust bowl, with no rain to water crops yet elsewhere floods were causing landslides with the loss of life, suffering, and further poverty. Crime continued to rise as the poor were forced to steal to feed their children.

The contrast to life on Mars was enormous. Here the colony worked together to build a peaceful city. The citizens were treated with dignity and all contributions were considered equally important. Working hours were balanced with leisure time and education was freely available.

Before the fourth anniversary, of the day they landed, the cousins met to discuss whether to stay for another two years.

"It's hard to imagine living on Earth now," Hamiora volunteered. "I don't know that I would want to live apart from Emma "

Hamiora had met Emma two years ago when she came to Mars with the second group of colonisers. A computer programmer with a wicked sense of humour, she was like a breath of fresh air.

"We would all miss her," Simone agreed. "I think we should stay on."

"I wish we could go back to visit everyone for Christmas and then come back."

Rose still had pangs of homesickness even though she talked frequently to family.

"Sounds like we're voting to stay."

Will rubbed his hands in satisfaction, eager to get on with what he'd planned.

One week after they'd made their decision, Simone received news that shocked and frightened her. She sent a text to her cousins to meet as soon as they were able, and they got together early that evening. They settled down in her bedroom and as she opened the memo, her hands trembled. The others had never seen Simone so disturbed.

She read from the screen.

"The population of Mars is being recalled. Get ready to leave immediately - The planet is to be used as a penal colony."

*'Take from the altars of the past
the fire – not the ashes.'*

Jean Jaures

Acknowledgements

The work involved in writing this book was not as difficult as keeping faith to the aim that others would enjoy reading it. The reason I was able to continue with it each day was because friends and family took the time to read it for me. The kind and helpful comments they made were invaluable.

I am indebted to you all, and to Terry Love, Sally Brown, Bev Wilson, Janine Jenness, Maria Hessman, and the late Laurie Wallace, and Doreen Corrick for allowing me to access family records.

When I began this project, I didn't consider the impact working on it would have on my partner.

However, it turned out he was a great help to me, suggesting words when I couldn't come up with the right one; listening to paragraphs I read out to him when I was uncertain about how I had described a scene.

He brought me endless cups of tea and, as the deadline drew closer, took over many of the household chores.

I could not have had a better companion. Thank you, Frank.